Behind the Mirror

BY VERLIE EVA MILLER

ILLUSTRATED BY JOYCE HERRINGSHAW

Inspiring Voices®
A Service of **Guideposts**

Copyright © 2012 Verlie Eva Miller.

All rights reserved. No part of this book may be used or reproduced by any means, graphic, electronic, or mechanical, including photocopying, recording, taping or by any information storage retrieval system without the written permission of the publisher except in the case of brief quotations embodied in critical articles and reviews.

Inspiring Voices books may be ordered through booksellers or by contacting:

Inspiring Voices
1663 Liberty Drive
Bloomington, IN 47403
www.inspiringvoices.com
1-(866) 697-5313

Because of the dynamic nature of the Internet, any web addresses or links contained in this book may have changed since publication and may no longer be valid. The views expressed in this work are solely those of the author and do not necessarily reflect the views of the publisher, and the publisher hereby disclaims any responsibility for them.

Any people depicted in stock imagery provided by Thinkstock are models, and such images are being used for illustrative purposes only.

Certain stock imagery © Thinkstock.

ISBN: 978-1-4624-0064-5 (sc)
ISBN: 978-1-4624-0063-8 (e)

Library of Congress Control Number: 2012931490

Printed in the United States of America

Inspiring Voices rev. date: 2/21/2012

The early part of the twentieth century often seems a very long time from the twenty-first century. In *Behind The Mirror* However, the differences in many ways seem only slight. The physical circumstances are often very different, but human nature is still the same in every century. We are reminded of patriotism and family ties, power and betrayal, of sin and need of repentance. There are longings and fulfillment, the power of compassion and love.

Verlie Eva Miller takes fascinating remembrances of her childhood and a series of incidents that were shared with her and weaves a tale of desperation and faith. This is an enticing story of the power of God working itself out in the lives of men, women and children, a mystery that is not resolved until the very end. The family roots originated in Finland and settled in northern Minnesota. It could happen anywhere or any time. It entertains, it challenges. Read and enjoy.

Beverly Brooks, MDiv

PREFACE

Behind the Mirror, flashed into my very being as I listened to a real life story. With only a skeleton of the facts, I longed to get out my scroll and dip my pen in a bottle of ink. The story that evolved and characters that I created have become my long, lost friends. I laughed through their triumphs and wept in their sorrows. With just a vein of truth to guide me, this story can only be classified as fiction. The setting is very familiar territory to me. I was born and spent the wonderful years of childhood and early marriage near Wadena.

After hearing the story, I spent one entire night wide awake, imagining what Hanna's life would be like. I regret not lighting my candle and beginning the story that night. The book would have doubled in content. It has been a long road to completion. My husband of sixty years suffered heart problems and surgeries. In spite of interruptions, I felt compelled to put my hand to the plow. I was deeply impressed that between the lines was a message for all who may read this book. Yes, one weak moment can change the entire course of our life.

I was born in 1924, the same year that I introduce Hanna Marie. Living in this period of history has been a positive contribution to my creativity. Join us around the parlor stove, and elevate your feet. Hanna will serve you a piping hot cup of tea and introduce you to our friends in the shadow *Behind the Mirror*.

Verlie Eva Miller

TABLE OF CONTENTS

CHAPTER 1	Home Again	1
CHAPTER 2	Mamma Goes Shopping	9
CHAPTER 3	Surprises	15
CHAPTER 4	Hanna Back in the Swing of Things	19
CHAPTER 5	Karly's Baptism	25
CHAPTER 6	Hanna Faces New Challenges	31
CHAPTER 7	The Walk That Made Memories	41
CHAPTER 8	Guardian Angels	49
CHAPTER 9	Childhood Left Behind	53
CHAPTER 10	Graduation	61
CHAPTER 11	College Days	71
CHAPTER 12	Heavy Decisions	75
CHAPTER 13	Lonely Days	81
CHAPTER 14	The Mail Box	91
CHAPTER 15	The Flowers Bloom	101
CHAPTER 16	Hanna Goes Traveling	107
CHAPTER 17	Time to Sew!	115
CHAPTER 18	The Wedding	123
CHAPTER 19	The Honeymoon	129
CHAPTER 20	Heidi and Karl	135
CHAPTER 21	Another Painful Good-bye	141
CHAPTER 22	More Adjustments	147
CHAPTER 23	The Great Unveiling	151

CHAPTER I

Home Again

Hanna Marie awoke with a guilty feeling as she looked at her alarm clock. *Oh, no! I wanted to surprise Mamma by making her a special breakfast,* she thought. *Why oh why did I sleep so long?* It was half past six.

Hanna Marie had placed a big white pitcher of water over the iron heat grate in the floor of her upstairs bedroom during the night so she could avoid an icy spits bath in the morning. Her elderly parents were up several times during the night to stoke the stove in the parlor. It was conveniently located just below Hanna Marie's bedroom. Having just arrived back home the day before, she now had her choice of bedrooms since all her siblings had evacuated the snug old nest. That morning, Hanna Marie hurriedly took care of her hygiene ritual. Then, after pulling her nine-patch quilt back to air, she opened the window a crack, intending to make her bed right after breakfast.

She smoothed the feather tick, and after dressing in a crisp, clean dress, she ran down the creaky, narrow stairs while tying her apron. The aroma of fresh-ground coffee and oatmeal penetrated the crack in the door at the foot of the stairway.

"Happy birthday, Mamma!" beamed Hanna.

Hanna Marie had been away for the past six years, except for a few holidays, and she had been unable to wish her mother a happy birthday except by letter. Today she could wish it to her verbally, since expressing her deep love and adoration with a big hug was a bit unnatural for these undemonstrative Finnish folk.

Sixteen years had elapsed since Papa, Hanna's beloved biological father, had received his eternal reward. It was still a little difficult for her to address Eli, the man who now filled the vacancy, as "Papa." The term applied to one and only one man. Papa and she had always been very close. Hanna Marie had been the apple of his eye. Calling Eli "Daddy" came a bit easier but not without strain and much practice at first.

Now that she had returned home after working in the big city for a number of years, she saw and felt anew the empty space that no man could ever fill: Papa's chair. It was positioned as though he might come in any minute, pick up the *Fergus Falls Journal*, and inevitably drop the paper in favor of an afternoon snooze.

"Mamma, I intended to be up early to prepare a surprise breakfast for you and...Daddy," forcing the word, but full knowing Daddy had earned it, as well as her respect and recognition.

Mamma was quick to respond. She smiled, with gratitude bursting from her eyes. "My land, I have been preparing breakfast for this family for so many years I can't count them."

Yes, Mamma was quite capable of frying potatoes, boiling

eggs, and cooking wheat that had been soaking overnight. She certainly was experienced.

Her daughter understood every word, though it was spoken in Finnish, Mamma's own native language. Mamma could not—or would not—speak in English even after living in America for twenty-four years. Perhaps being a perfectionist was the motivating factor behind it all. Mamma could understand every word, but if she could not speak English perfectly, she would stick to her own mother tongue.

It was 1901 when the Heikkinen family sailed from their homeland. The sojourners included the eldest boys, Jussel and Pekka (twin brothers who later became known as John and Peter to non-Finnish neighbors), along with their twin sisters, Krata and Marta, and little two-year-old Hanna Marie. Their parents, Greta and Ade, completed the immigrant family. Hanna Marie was not sure if she could remember the long trip or if she had simply heard the story so many times that she thought she remembered every detail.

They left their birth country to seek a better life for their growing family. Papa had recognized that the portion of land he had inherited in their native Finland was not sufficient. He and his five brothers worked tirelessly, endeavoring to eke out a living on adjoining plots in their beloved homeland, but the outlook for success was growing less and less favorable. They must improve their prospects elsewhere.

Ade was adventurous, and with a spouse who was just as willing, they took off for the land of milk and honey. Weighing carefully the treasures they could pack in an old family trunk was difficult to say the least. Saying farewell to friends and family was the final test, knowing a great ocean might very well separate them forever. They questioned their own wisdom, not to mention sanity, when heavy storms tossed their ship for hours.

Verlie Eva Miller

That very trunk was now the highly prized possession of Hanna Marie. She had just moved back home with all her worldly belongings—and secrets—contained in the old trunk, now situated in a dark corner of the attic. It held captive things she had collected for housekeeping during the years she had lived in the big city of Minneapolis. A few treasured letters and pictures that she had no intention of sharing with anyone had been placed on the very top of the trunk. It was locked, and no one would ever discover where she had hidden the key.

Living in the big city had its temporary amusements. Hot and cold running water and gas lights at her fingertips were delightful novelties. However, working at a factory during World War I was not what it was cracked up to be. The hours were long and tedious. Hanna lived on the third floor of a stately house and dearly missed the big farmhouse, especially its beloved occupants. However she admittedly cherished payday, carefully following the advice of her mother to tuck away all she could for her dream home. Hanna spent her share of moments in reverie, thinking of that ideal home, yet nonetheless daunted by the realization, *I am twenty-four years old with no sign of my knight in shining armor. Will I ever find him?* Her heart would sink with regret.

She was now convinced her only choice was to move home. The children were all grown now and had established homes of their own. Mamma had suffered heart problems, and other circumstances now beyond Hanna's control found her back in Mamma's kitchen on this cool spring day.

"Mamma, I will do up all the dishes, milk separator and pails. I want you go to town with Daddy and pick out some fabric, and I will make you a new dress." Hanna handed her mother an envelope with a hand-designed card containing precious little morsels that described her feelings better than all the cards in the five and dime; Hanna had a way

Behind the Mirror

with words. Enclosed in the card were two of Hanna Marie's hard-earned dollars. Mamma read the card with an earnest expression and gently reached for her apron skirt to dry a tear that made its way down her cheek.

"Thank you, Hanna Marie," she uttered as she tried to clear her throat and regain her composure. "You're so thoughtful. I could really use a new dress for church and special occasions, but you should save your money."

Mamma rubbed the two dollar bills together and held them out to Hanna to no avail. With her large family there had always been a grain binder needing a part, a young one— or a horse—needing shoes, and Greta had cheerfully placed her needs and desires near the bottom of the list through the years. She was meticulous with her best dresses, but still they did deteriorate with age.

Mamma recalled her favorite dress that her mother had made for her wedding in Finland. It was now in the attic keeping the old trunk company. She could not throw it away. Whenever she went to the attic she reached under the yellowing sheet just to feel the satin. Pausing to take a trip down memory lane always brought Ade close to her. She could feel the warmth and weight of his arm around her. Years could not rob her of those precious, newlywed days. She had made a number of dresses over the years, many maternity, and always of calico or cotton.

Hanna was only nine years old when Papa went to his eternal home. It was the end of the harvest, and it had been a bumper crop that year.

"It is going to snow soon, and that corn has to be in the crib for winter feeding," Ade had said.

Think ahead and be prepared, that was the cry of Papa's heart. Greta knew arguing the point was useless, though Ade had been up most of the night drinking hot tea with an unhealthy cough, continually stoking the fire. As dusk closed in, he staggered into the house too sick to remove his frozen clothes. Greta scolded him as she unbuttoned his denim jacket.

"Ade, why did you stay out until you were so exhausted?" she asked.

She knew the answer to her question. She understood the struggles he faced to keep the farm afloat.

Pekka ran to the nearest neighbors. He knocked on the door before rushing in. "Papa is real sick," he blurted out forgetting his usual greeting. Mr. Scott dressed for a cold trip, harnessed the horses to the sleigh, and they were off to fetch the doctor.

After a hurried explanation, Dr. Croft grabbed his worn bag and hopped on the sleigh, dressed in his sheepskin coat and his felt shoes inside his over-boots. The red geldings, sensing the urgency of the situation, raised their heads into the rough elements and responded to their master's firm, "Get up."

"His lungs are congested beyond remedy. It will be a miracle if he pulls through," Dr. Croft confessed after examining Ade.

Ade did not respond to the medication. On Sunday night the elders were called in to pray, their wives bringing supper for the anxious family. The children ate and then tiptoed to the bedroom wall, listening intently to the prayer that ascended, adding petitions of their own.

Ade died that night. No one was sure why God did not honor those prayers. Greta pondered this for many years. Could it have been lack of faith, or was it sin that short-circuited their requests? Why would God allow her helpmate, her lover, her husband, and the father of her children to be snatched away from her?

They had only been in the States eight years. During this time Ade had worked hard clearing and tilling the new land.

Behind the Mirror

He built the farm buildings, machine sheds, chicken coops, and hog barns. In addition, he even constructed a sauna and a playhouse for Hanna and her new baby sister. The members of the Heikkinen family were now new citizens of the United States of America.

Ade's woodworking skill was displayed throughout the Red Country Church where, in his wedding suit, he now lay in a homemade casket. His tall body was stretched out near the altar and cross that bespoke his craftsmanship. The little church was crowded with mourners, the first two rows filled with his bereaved family.

These little ones will never know their Father, Greta thought as she held the tiniest of their two children born since they arrived in America; they were unaware of their great loss.

Ade now rested from all his labors. His sleep had always been peaceful, as only a righteous man could enjoy. Greta was comforted as the deep voice of Oscar Lang sang, "Safe In the Arms of Jesus." Yet she herself longed to be cradled in the arms of her own gallant lover. Still she determined to go on. Where there is a will, there is a woman. She must not falter.

Hanna's stepfather interrupted this blessed flood of memories and entered the house with two shotgun pails of milk. He nodded good-day to Hanna as Greta stepped aside from her kitchen range to strain the fresh milk through a thin dishtowel. Eli removed his boots and jacket. The warmth of the kitchen now mingled with the cold air, and the aroma of breakfast with the odor from the cattle. Likewise, sunny thoughts mingled with a dark cloud—a secret cloud—that hung over the household that crisp morning. While these stoic souls would not allow themselves the freedom to speak a word of it, they could not conceal their crestfallen countenance. This mystery was a subject they vowed they would never speak of and passionately hoped the world they lived in would never discover.

CHAPTER 2

Mamma Goes Shopping

After breakfast, Hanna Marie stood in the doorway until the buggy was out of sight. She was thinking of Mamma and the heavy load she bore over the years. For Mamma there was never a dull moment, rarely a minute for reflection. Mamma sat still only long enough to darn socks, patch knees in britches, and sew diapers for her ever-expanding family. Hanna pondered the toll that a constant grind had taken on Mamma's health, leading to her heart attack, and she shuddered to think of another daunting circumstance which might have contributed to her suffering as well.

A cold shiver reminded Hanna to close the door and

tend the fires. *Oh, my! I had forgotten how I hated this pesky job of washing all the milk dishes and pails.* It was a morning and evening daily chore that Hanna had abhorred. Day after day Mamma had done this task without a murmur.

Hanna glanced in the small looking glass over the kitchen knick-knack shelf. She was more beautiful than she realized. Papa was the person that had often reminded her of that fact. At eight years of age her hair hung in ringlets around her pretty face, and her shy but sparkling eyes could light up any room. Hanna Marie could still hear his thrilling words as though it were yesterday, "Oh, my little rose."

Even during the awkward years of adolescence Papa's words echoed in her soul. Little sisters soon took center stage, and Hanna Marie vanished into the woodwork after the death of Papa. Along with the older siblings, she shared the busy tasks of keeping the household running smoothly, and no one seemed to notice, least of all Hanna herself, that she was maturing into a beautiful young woman.

During these years, Greta faced her widowhood as a brave soldier. Jussel and Pekka were trained cattlemen. The cows were milked, watered, and fed. The barn was cleaned before the boys headed across the frozen lake to school. In spring and fall they took the road, traversing around the lake. Each member of the house was assigned daily tasks. Greta praised her little maids for work well done as she trained and coached their performance when it did not meet her standard.

Eli, a bachelor neighbor, lived a couple miles down the road. Barely a year after he and his wife had left their homeland in Finland to settle in America, he, too, suffered a tragic loss—the death of his wife and newborn son during childbirth. Eli's grief shut him up in his home as a hermit, but when he learned of Ade's untimely death, his heart was awakened to the suffering of this large family. A desire to

Behind the Mirror

help and comfort surfaced and nudged him out the door, past his own grief, to offer the only thing he had to give, charity in the form of practical help. A day or two after Ade's passing, Eli came over to finish what Ade had started that cold day he died. After he unloaded the last of the corn, Eli knocked on the door and opened it a crack to say, "If there is anything else I can do, please send one of the boys for me."

Greta thanked him. As she closed the door she muttered to herself, "He is very kind, but the last thing I want to do is appear to attach myself to anyone. And I certainly don't want to start the rumor mill circulating. No," she sighed, "with my big boys and girls, we will manage somehow." Independent from the time she was a toddler buckling her own shoes, she was now more self-determined than ever. She vowed she would never consider marriage again. How could she forget her first love?

Eli went home from the Heikkinen's that day in better spirits than he had been in years. Helping this needy family lifted the sorrow he had been enduring for this long while. He waited patiently for them to respond.

By the time spring rolled around Greta admitted that the boys should not miss school to plow and seed. Taking Eli's offer more seriously, she discussed it with Hanna. They agreed that if Eli's willingness to help still stood, they must avail themselves of his kindness. The big brothers were so steeped in their workload that they were too busy to take the time to even speak with Eli about it, so Hanna took immediate action and was off to Eli's homestead. The sun was melting the snow so fast that streams were running down the muddy trail. Eli came to the door with the newspaper in his hand and his glasses resting low on his nose.

"Why Hanna you have grown so much, I could barely recognize you when I saw you coming down the trail." Eli's dog, Old Shag, continued to bark. It had been a month of

Verlie Eva Miller

Sundays since a female had set foot in the house. "I guess I had dozed off while reading the paper, but Old Shag here saw you coming," he fairly shouted over Shag's excitement.

Hanna was one to get to the point. "Mamma was wondering if you would have time to do some plowing and help the boys put in the crops this spring?" Eli laid down his paper and glasses on the cluttered table and offered Hanna a chair as he brushed the crumbs on the floor.

"I would be very pleased to help the boys," he said eagerly. "I seeded most of my land into alfalfa, so I do not have any urgent work this spring."

"How much would you charge per day if you use our team and machinery?" Hanna asked.

Looking around she could not help but see that Eli needed a housekeeper. "Or perhaps we could barter?" she quickly added, secretly hoping to save Mamma some cash.

"I certainly could use help around here," Eli admitted.

The deal was finalized and the little businesswoman could hardly wait to break the news. She went flying down the hill with her curly hair flowing straight back. Her eyes lit up as blue as the sky.

The crops did get in. It was 1910, and lack of rain stunted the harvest that year. Although the crops were disappointing, other seeds were sown that would lend a joyful harvest for Greta.

Since returning to her childhood home, Hanna was constantly recalling bygone years. She shook herself back to reality. *Right now I must get to the duties at hand and try to dismiss the past.*

Soon Mamma's little terrier, Duffy, began to bark to go outside. Just as Hanna opened the door, Myrna was clenching her fist to knock. Hanna startled and backed away. She was not expecting, nor desiring visitors; it was early in the day. Truth be told, she was not eager to speak with anyone yet

Behind the Mirror

since returning to the farm, least of all Myrna. Hanna Marie had important things on her mind, things that she could not share with anyone.

"Well, Hanna Marie!" exclaimed Myrna loudly. "Land sakes, I certainly never expected you to be home. Where is Greta?"

Myrna was adept at asking more questions in sequence than any listener could possibly answer. In this case, it proved to Hanna's advantage. She could choose which queries she preferred to address and which she would drop.

"How long are you going to be home? I hear you really have a good job. I hope you aren't going to give that up. Land sakes, you have changed since I saw you last. It must have been more than a year. Greta never said a word about you coming home. Funny she didn't tell me."

Myrna became lightly offended whenever she wasn't privy to all the news of her friends' lives. She took a deep breath to show her annoyance, and unbuttoned her coat.

"May I take your wraps?" offered Hanna. "Won't you have a chair, Myrna? Mamma went along to town. It is her birthday today."

"Oh, I know it is her birthday!" relieved that she knew that much. "That is the reason for my call."

Myrna pulled cookies wrapped in a napkin from her pocket; she had hoped that Greta would share a birthday tea.

Lord, help me to be considerate, and please bless her with brevity, Hanna prayed silently. Myrna was a kind soul but curious, or was it that Myrna was so bored that she had to stick her nose in the lives of every resident within a fifty-mile radius?

Hanna put the teakettle on and stirred up the fire in the range. Mamma's best china was placed on the dining room table along with crisp linens. Myrna's fresh sugar cookies were admittedly delicious. Duffy barked to join the tea party. Hanna excused herself and opened the door. The dog darted in, growling at the neighbor.

As fussy as Greta is, I can't believe that she would allow that crotchety dog in the house, thought Myrna, an opinion she saw fit to air and share with several neighbors later that very day.

"I hope Mamma gets home soon, but a horse and buggy only go so fast," she sighed. "Besides, it takes time to pick out just the right fabric and thread." She spoke primarily to herself as she pulled back the muslin curtain and looked longingly down the dirt road as far as her eyes would take her. Hanna was oh so sincere in expressing her desire for their return. *When will I be released from Myrna's continual interrogation*, she wondered? Her answer came quickly.

"Well, I can't wait any longer. Please convey my best wishes to Greta. Thank you for the tea, and when will you be going back to the cities?" Myrna was building up a blizzard of questions.

"Land a livin' what I wouldn't have given for a job like yours, during a depression like we have. Did you know you have a dish towel on the line that is just a whippin' to pieces?"

"Yes, I know I hung the strainer out there. It needs to whip."

Myrna left abruptly and Duffy gave out another growl. Hanna patted the dog approvingly. She was now content to have a moment to herself. "Oh! My window is open and I haven't even made my bed!"

Hanna wanted everything in tip-top order so she could begin sewing Mamma's dress by the afternoon. She felt a tinge of pride in the knowledge that she had successfully dodged the worst of Myrna's questions, at least the most dreaded ones.

CHAPTER 3

Surprises

Hanna Marie rushed upstairs to her well-aired room. She hadn't intended on leaving her bed unmade more than a few minutes. Having a tidy, scrupulous mother like Greta, Hanna had learned to take pride in her housekeeping. Once her bed was made, she flew down the steps, two at a time, determined to have lunch all ready for Mamma and Daddy when they returned at noon.

It did not take long for Hanna to get back into the swing of things when it came to homemaking. It was always simple meals that graced the table.

Mamma deserves a cake on her birthday, she thought. The old recipe book was battered and torn. There were a few recipes tucked in a brown envelope, written in Finnish in

Verlie Eva Miller

Grandmother's handwriting. Though faded from age, Hanna could read them. Making sure the oven would be hot, she added more wood before combining the ingredients. As the cake baked, she scrubbed three potatoes that Eli had stowed in the cellar the previous fall. The aroma from the ten-gallon crock of sauerkraut in the corner of the cellar sharpened her appetite. Pickled beets and dill added the final touches. Frosting was made as the cake was cooling.

Greta and Eli drove in just as the tooth picks and salt and pepper were placed in the center of the table. Hanna peeked through the dotted-Swiss curtain from the dining room.

Mamma was carefully assisted as she alighted the buggy. Hanna longed for the day to come that she would experience such tender care and respect. Daddy backed the buggy into the shed. Then he led the team to the tank for a drink of water. "You're likely as hungry as I am," Eli groaned as he threw a fork full of hay in the manger. The horses snorted as they nibbled at their allotment of oats dumped into the bins which had been chewed down by Barney and Queen; they had either been bored, or perhaps low on some mineral like copper.

"I am starved," Eli admitted as he pulled off his boots and jacket. By this time Greta had changed into her everyday clothes and faded apron. With the Depression and Hoover as President, she was grateful to have a change of clothes, a roof over her head, and food on her plate. The front page of the *Fergus Falls Journal* displayed growing numbers of hungry people in the bread lines.

Greta was pleased as punch over the bargains to be had in the nearby town of Sebeka. She not only found fabric for a dress, but also for a matching apron, thread, buttons, and bias tape. For once, she spent her entire birthday gift.

"Thank you Hanna Marie. I know you worked hard for that money," said Mamma with beaming eyes.

Behind the Mirror

Hanna never discussed her savings, but had a comfortable feeling that she would not be a burden to her parents. She knew home, this home, was now where she belonged.

"Remember what the Doctor said, now Greta, and take your nap," Eli urged when the meal was finished. Yes, it was resting time for both of them. Eli worried about Greta with her heart condition. He curled up in Ade's old chair and was soon snoring. Hanna was grateful for Daddy Eli, and she determined to embrace the sight of him in Papa's chair. Yet, as dear as he was, he could never fill Papa's shoes.

While Mamma and Daddy settled in for their naps, Hanna quickly called her brother Jussel and his wife, Anna. "Can you come over tonight for birthday cake about seven? I have it hidden in the pantry. How is the baby?" she asked, admitting to herself she that was even more eager to see her new nephew, than her brother and his wife.

"Oh yes, we can. I am excited to show you our precious little bundle. He has been a little fussy at night, so we will not be able to stay long.We will do the chores a little earlier, and we'll see you at seven." Anna and Jussel had waited six long years for this little Karl Thomas.

Hanna spread the fabric on the dining room table. She then found a pattern in the sewing machine drawer that she could adjust to fit Mamma since she had lost twenty pounds. How generously Mamma had given of her time and talent over the years for stacks of garments that her nimble hands had fashioned. Hanna Marie was looking forward to relieving Mamma of her duties, yet Mamma never seemed to feel the weight of the burden. She performed her tasks with a spirit of love that made the load seem light.

Having given birth to two more children after they arrived in America and then another child after her marriage to Eli, was it any wonder she was tired? Early one morning a few weeks before Hanna returned home, Mamma's "old ticker gave way." The doctor diagnosed it as light heart attack.

Eli was just returning from the evening chores when Jussel drove in with his 1926 Ford. He was proud of his car, but much more excited about the baby in Anna's arms. Hanna Marie rushed to the door to catch a glimpse of her nephew. Anna walked over to the table and unveiled her pride and joy. Greta sat in her rocker wishing her entire family was close enough to join this very special party.

"May I hold him?" asked Auntie Hanna Marie.

"Of course." Anna's kind eyes detected the deep desire Hanna tried, but failed, to conceal. How she longed for a baby of her own, and how well Anna herself understood that yearning.

Hanna picked him up gently and held him close to her heart. She opened his tiny hand, and he wrapped it around her finger. Her heart melted and tears welled in her eyes. Hanna wondered silently, *could anything be more precious? Will I ever have a child I can call my very own?* At that moment the prospects did not look bright. She vowed she would enjoy baby Karl every moment she could. Someday, perhaps God in his grace will allow her to share the joy of real motherhood with a life partner.

CHAPTER 4

Hanna Back in the Swing of Things

How time changes things, mused Hanna Marie while wrestling with a sheet against a breeze as she reached for a clothespin. The South wind assured her that the snow-white wash would dry softly in God's great outdoors. A year ago she was working in the big city of Minneapolis. She never dreamed she would move back home and take Mamma's place. Mamma would certainly be proud of the delightful sight of the hanging wash against the background of the purple lilac bushes. There was a clear blue sky over head.

I am sure Mamma is looking out the window, Hanna almost uttered audibly.

Through the years Mamma's instructions were explicit. Hanna could recite them in her sleep. "Be sure to hang like articles together, and *always* hang the underwear on the back line. If you need more space, just put the boys' overalls on the back fence."

Hanna recalled the earlier days when the wash was carried down the hill to the sandy beach of the lake. The little ones would splash around on the shallow lakeshore while Hanna and the twins assisted with the washing. Their job was to keep a good supply of fresh rinse water for Mamma and hang the wet clothes back at the farmyard. Wet overalls, too heavy for the little girls to carry, were sometimes thrown over the branches of a nearby tree to dry. Blackberries, wild raspberries, and chokecherries would be picked as the seasons produced them along the banks of the creek.

Yes, things had changed. Hanna Marie now washed with a wooden washer and a hand wringer. *How did Mamma ever wring those sheets out by hand?*

Hanna was right. Greta was indeed looking out the window. She would never think of ruffling the stiffly starched curtains, allowing Hanna to know she was spying.

Greta recalled the endless task of changing diapers. How she longed for the energy just to carry a wicker basket filled with baby flannels. While staring out the window, pleasant memories surfaced and brought her children closer.

Hanna Marie swung the empty basket and strolled back to the house. The air was so fresh compared to the smoky city. She breathed deeply before entering the door to find Mamma conveniently sitting at her White sewing machine, working on her fan pattern quilt blocks. Her quilts were museum quality, never a hanging thread, with patterns and corners perfectly matched and carefully pressed. Mamma found joy in quilting and relished colorful and exuberant fabrics.

"Mamma, I would like to go over to Jussel and Anna's before dinner," Hanna declared.

Hanna had been home for a week and was so busy getting settled into the routine of homemaking that she had not taken the time to visit a brother who lived only a half mile away. As she walked, she paused to listen to the melting snow rush down the hill to a creek below and noticed the cowslips peeking through behind an old stump. She could not resist gathering a few for Anna. A woodpecker was keeping perfect time as he pecked at a tree, pausing only to see if that pretty maid was a threat to his project.

Oh, I did not know how to appreciate the sounds and fragrance of spring, until I lived in a smoky, noisy city for all those years. She sighed and took another deep breath. She hurried on to surprise Anna, aware that Jussel would be out working.

"Come in," Anna responded to the knock. Anna was in the bedroom tucking baby Karly in his cradle. It was the same cradle in which Hanna Marie's little sister had slept. Papa created it from leftover cabinet scraps. The sight of the old cradle along with its precious contents brought tears to Hanna's eyes.

Hanna Marie held Karly for a spell and then gently placed him back in his snug bed. Anna admired the cowslips, while putting them in a vase and then made tea.

After a time, Hanna glanced at the cuckoo clock on Anna's wall. "Well, I must get home. Mamma will finish dinner if I don't show up, and she is just apt to check the clothes on the line. Whenever you need help with little Karl, please be sure to let me know." Her eyes bespoke a longing in her soul.

As usual, Hanna Marie fairly flew home. She was sure she was born in a hurry. It was an often stated fact, and a highly regaled joke, that the midwife back in Finland who delivered her was "rushin.'" She paused briefly to gather cowslips for

Verlie Eva Miller

Mamma. Hanna had dinner in the oven, but trusted Mamma to add fuel to the fire in the old, black kitchen range.

Will I ever have the pleasure of filling Papa's crib with a replica of Papa? That was the million dollar question that secretly came to Hanna's mind as she hurried home. The ever-ready answer that surfaced was: *You have neither a prospect nor a boyfriend, much less a husband.*

Her duty now was to lighten Mamma's load and be content *in whatsoever state* she was in. *I suppose that includes the state of Minnesota,* she laughed to herself. She vowed she was going to see little Karly every day. It would be a welcomed break from the daily chores. She often breathed a prayer for strength and the courage to fulfill her calling.

As Hanna Marie trudged along home through the fields and past Eli's old home place, memories surfaced. She recalled the day she made the deal with him to exchange her work with Eli's expertise on farming, never dreaming as she cleaned every nook and corner of his home that it was the beginning of the romance between Mamma and Daddy Eli.

She had known Eli as a quiet, secluded bachelor until the day after papa died when he came and unloaded the wagon of corn that Papa had just picked. Because of the sorrow he had quietly endured for several years, that good deed seemed to draw him back to the long-forgotten man he had once been. The old house looked lonely now. It was crying for paint or even a little linseed oil.

Just over the hill a little boy was buried in the arms of his mother, and with them, all of Eli's dreams. He went on only by burying himself in farm work. He spent as little time as possible between the walls of silence that reminded him of his sorrow.

The working relationship between Eli and the Heikkinen had happened so naturally. Eli was thrilled to be needed, Hanna's big brothers responded to his advice, and the little sisters worked their way to the softest part of Eli's heart. However, going back home in the evening was progressively lonelier for Eli each night, though he certainly appreciated crawling into bed between the snow-white sheets his little maid diligently washed, dried, starched, and ironed.

The rooms were now dust-free and the walls freshly painted. The cowslips were arranged in the one and only vase that survived the trip from Finland and placed in the center of the table on the freshly ironed tablecloth. The back wooden porch was scrubbed with brush and lye water. Whenever he entered the house, Eli scraped every blade of grass off, along with any farm residue, from his work boots and then exchanged them for his bedroom slippers. *That little makeshift housewife will scold if I don't*, he would laugh to himself.

The starched curtains hung straight, and the old shades were removed, scrubbed and repaired. Eli noticed them as he strolled home one night. Hanna had even sewn new seams for the slats. *That Hanna Marie amazes me to no end. Now why didn't I at least cut the ragged things all one length?* To be honest with himself, his heart was so broken he forgot he even had shades, nor did he care at the time.

Hanna's walk down this well-worn memory lane gave way to reality as she returned home to discover that Mamma had fallen asleep in her chair. The wind had decided to change directions, whipping the wash around the line. Eli was just pulling up with the team and wagon from town. Hanna Marie had best hurry in to put the finishing touches on dinner. The aroma of the pork roast and sauerkraut was mouthwatering. *I wouldn't be surprised if that old north wind blew in the neighbors for dinner*, Hanna thought.

CHAPTER 5

Karly's Baptism

Dreams of having a child had nearly faded before the adoption. It had seemed an impossibility to Anna and Jussel. When little Karl was finally placed in their family, it took time to adjust to the duties of parenthood, but it was with gratitude that they approached the long-awaited privilege.

Anna and Jussel spent hours talking of dreams they had for baby Karly. That their son would be grounded in their Lutheran upbringing went without saying, and through faith and prayers God would become real to him, securing a place in little Karl's heart and future. They would faithfully teach him the Bible stories that had shaped their own lives.

Anna's pain of infertility was shared with mothers in Bible times. The stories of Hannah, Samuel's mother, Elisabeth, John the Baptist's mother, and Rebecca, Isaac's mother had been of great comfort to Anna. Could it be that God chose these women to raise godly leaders, women who cried out to Him to ease the pain of their empty arms? Grateful parents are the best of parents. They know how to pray because they hold in their arms the answer to their prayers. They know their duty, as well.

"We must have Karly baptized," Anna reminded Jussel. "We will set the date very soon."

Verlie Eva Miller

On the next visit from Hanna Marie, Anna met her at the door with a question.

"Oh, Hanna would you consider making a baptismal gown for Karly?"

Hanna beamed as she took off her shawl and stocking cap. It was early June, but a cool north wind was a reminder that this was Minnesota. Papa had always warned his children, "Never leave home unprepared for winter."

The teakettle was singing a familiar invitation for a cup of spring tea. Anna could almost set the clock by Hannah Marie's midmorning visit. Their relationship grew like the petunias in her garden. Anna loved the break in the day that brought her sister by marriage. They were as close as two sisters could be. Anna missed her childhood friends back in Michigan, and Hanna determined to make up for that loss and become her kindred spirit.

While the tea was brewing, Anna described the gown she pictured for baby Karl.

"You know, I think Mamma has just the material we need." Hanna recalled the last baby Mamma gave birth to that never made it to the crib. Separated from the womb prematurely, he went directly to his heavenly home. The fabric for his gown had been purchased a few weeks before he was due. Of course Mamma did not know if she would make it with lace and frills or not. The little one concluded all of Greta's labor pains, soon buried in her sorrow. Having given birth to girls for the past few deliveries, she felt another part of her heart was beneath the sod behind the Red Country Church. The satin material was tucked away, along with the buttons and thread in the bottom bureau drawer.

"How long before you need the gown?" asked Hanna.

"I must call Reverend Spicer before I can answer that question."

Hanna Marie rushed home as though the service would

Behind the Mirror

be tomorrow. She thought soberly of asking Mamma if it would be permissible to make use of that material. Perhaps she would be opening old wounds.

Well, now that I have volunteered, I must go through the painful steps before cutting into that sacred fabric, Hanna told herself.

Not waiting to check to see if Mamma would be resting, Hanna Marie rushed in the house and caught Mamma snoozing in her rocker.

"Mamma, I want you to be very honest with me. Would you care to make good use of the cloth you saved for baby Jon? Anna requested I sew a gown for Karly."

Mamma shook her head to be sure she was awake before making a foolish decision.

"Hanna, my dear! I could never have thought of a better idea. It has been a comfort to me over the years, but now I feel it will not be long before I see baby Jon in his heavenly robe." Mamma was also sensitive to the fact that Anna and Jussel may be short of funds.

Dinner was soon on the table and Daddy, Mamma, and the cook sat down to sausage, boiled red potato, and rutabagas with some hard rolls to complete the meal.

"You should see how that baby has grown. He changes every day. He smiled at me today! I can't wait to get started with his gown," expressed Hanna.

Mamma wiped the dishes during their favorite subject of discussion: Baby Karl. Greta did have more grandchildren, but they were past the baby stage and long past hiking the half-mile to where Karl lived. No one had the wherewithal to take long trips or even to take many pictures during a depression. Nevertheless, Greta would not forget her other offspring; she named everyone of them in her daily prayers and longed to see them more often than the distance that separated them allowed.

Verlie Eva Miller

How wonderful to at last know that her eldest son was now as proud a father as any papa could be. He had to admit that Karly bore a strange resemblance to both he and Anna, yet everyone in the neighborhood was aware that he was adopted. He also knew that neighbors did not have the least idea of the adoption agency. They had their application sent to every source they could locate before the surprise baby arrived, so the details remained a mystery.

On the day of the baptism, Hanna Marie sat with the other relatives in the second row of the small church. She was dressed in her very best black dress and hat. The whole township was excited about this service. How thrilling for Hanna to think she had sewn every stitch in that gown. Baby Karl peeked out over Anna's shoulder as though he was looking directly at his seamstress. His red hair and fair skin stood out like a rose. Hanna Marie was sure she detected a faint smile, though admitting her keen eyesight was sometimes enhanced by a vivid imagination.

The service was touching. There were very few dry eyes in the sanctuary. Hanna hoped no one noticed how wet her handkerchief was.

The Ross twins were also baptized that day. It was a holy ceremony. Hanna prayed that somehow baby Karl would know how sincere his parents were about his godly inheritance. Again, Hanna's mind wandered to her buried desires to be standing before God with a precious bundle of her own one day.

While Daddy was untying the horses from the post, Hanna helped Mamma into the buggy then loaded the step stool that Mamma now needed in order to climb in. Barney and Queen were soon trotting on home to their reward, the delightful taste of alfalfa.

Hanna was rather quiet on the way home. Mamma attempted dialogue, but any subject she introduced was pensively dismissed. Hanna headed up the stairs as she bid goodnight to Mamma and Daddy. Somehow she needed a moment of silence. She completed her nightly rituals and crawled into her cozy bed. Sleep was deferred until she had renewed her covenant with God to be content to be a nursemaid until He had other plans for her life.

She awoke the next morning refreshed and the spirit within her renewed. Mamma was waiting for Hanna Marie to assist with her bath, and Hanna was ready now to talk about any subject Mamma's little heart desired.

Little Karl was the continual topic of the day for five more years. He grew as the garden each year and was the delight of Grandpa and Grandma, and Hanna fairly worshipped him.

CHAPTER 6

Hanna Faces New Challenges

Hanna Marie worked tirelessly through the years since moving back home. The church was just beginning Bible classes for children, and Hanna Marie's heart warmed at the thought of teaching the truths of the Scripture to these precious, moldable young minds.

"Come in Mr. Wind," Greta called, thinking it was only the strong breeze banging the storm door. To her surprise in walked the parson. Greta quickly slipped off her apron as she arose from her rocker.

"I am sorry to just barge in like this," he apologized. "I was just on my way home from Myrna's. Her husband, Ralph, has been ill for the past few days."

The parson took a deep breath while wiping the sweat from his brow. "Hanna Marie, you are just the person I want to see. We are preparing to start a Sunday School. Knowing your love of children, you were the first candidate that came to my mind."

Hanna Marie did not have to think twice before consenting. She did, however, have many questions. With Karl in mind, she quickly volunteered. "May I teach the first graders?"

"Well, I think we could work that out. You know we have a growing crew of children and limited space, so we may have to double up classes." He stroked his mustache as he continued, "But those are good challenges, and I'm sure we can resolve them." The parson spoke in broken English. He did not need an interpreter to understand Greta in their own native language.

"Please tell me, Reverend Spicer, how is Ralph this morning?" asked Hanna.

"He is improving and the Doctor is confident that his body will mend. We are calling the elders to pray with him tonight. I don't know what we would do without Ralph in this community. He's everyone's 'Mr. Fix-all.'"

As the parson turned to go, Hanna assured him she would be at the first teachers' meeting. As she closed the door, she burst into laughter.

"Oh, Mamma, I can hardly wait to teach those children," she exclaimed.

There were no classroom divisions in the old, musty basement, but one corner was assigned for the little tots. Hanna walked to the church to prepare the room and found that the the walls had to be swept first with a stiff broom. She was happy to find other enthusiastic workers there as well. Paint was scraped from the windows before they could be pried open. An anonymous donor responded to the need,

Behind the Mirror

and a new coat of paint would freshen the stone walls and the cement floor.

Jussel was consulted about the division for Hanna Marie's classroom.

"Well, I have a few two-by-fours left over from the shed I built. I think we could frame a divider. Don't know what we can use for the walls."

Hanna rushed on home to prepare supper and solve that problem. The following day Hanna accompanied Daddy to Sebeka to select some material for a curtain for her basement windows. A winter supply of warp for rugs was also a necessity on her list, as Hanna's skill in rug weaving was becoming well known throughout the county. When she alighted the buggy she noticed a very large cardboard box being carried into a furniture store.

"Daddy do not untie the horses yet, I must go in this store." Daddy knew she did not have money for a stick of furnishings, but obliging as usual, he walked back to the buggy.

"Say, Mr. Wallingford, what do you plan to do with the large piece of cardboard?" He sensed an immediate need in Hanna Marie's voice. "I have a wall division started and nothing to complete the job. It's for my Sunday School classroom. Jussel framed the room in."

A few minutes later, a smiling twosome were scattering dust as they rolled along with a load of cardboard tied to the side of the buggy. Kind Mr. Wallingford even donated the nails to complete the job.

"We may as well drop it off at the church," Hanna suggested.

By sundown the two walls were covering the frame. Hanna was so enthusiastic that she almost covered the doorframe that Jussel had made. She was grinning from ear to ear as she stepped back to admire the project. "Now

Verlie Eva Miller

Lord, help me to find something to cover these old cardboard walls."

Earlier, Hanna moved old church records from the basement to the attic. "No one will ever miss these musty, old records, and besides, they will be much safer up here," she muttered to herself as she climbed a rickety ladder, endeavoring to clear her conscience for not first consulting the elders. An old notebook slipped from her grasp.

She stooped to pick it up after depositing the rest of her load in the attic. Leafing through the pages, Ade Heikkinen's name stood out as though in bold print.

Ade Heikkinen completed the woodwork and a cross in the front of the pulpit area and constructed the altar. Hanna Marie read on and on, lost in a sea of memories. "Oh, Papa, I see the work of your blessed hands every where I look."

She paused to kneel before the altar and gazed at the cross that her dear Papa had created. Wiping away the tears while making her final trip to the attic, she stopped and glanced at the clock on the back of the church and gasped, "How could time get away from me?"

Hanna slept, ate, and drank Sunday School as the summer days slipped by, barely knowing she was weeding or harvesting. She was divinely inspired and her enthusiasm proved contagious.

"Now I have another special calling besides rug-making and gardening to keep me happy as an old maid," she said to Mamma.

"Hanna Marie, now hush! I know God has someone special for you. I hope he is the handsome fellow I saw in my dream last night," Mamma confessed. Mamma described the details of that dream, and Hanna rehearsed it in her own daydreams in the years to come.

"Mamma, you are such a dreamer. I think I am destined

Behind the Mirror

to be a carpet weaver and a Sunday School teacher forever," Hanna Marie continued.

Well, whatever she was destined to be, she vowed she would put her whole heart into her project. It was not a difficult assignment to teach these lovable little children. The stories became very much alive in their curious minds. Acting out the Bible stories was the highlight of each Sunday.

"I would like to be the donkey," Karly volunteered excitedly.

The Good Samaritan shelled out a few buttons and stones to pay the Inn Keeper and promised to pay all expenses. One poor, lifeless boy hung as dead weight on Karly's back. It was a story they would remember for a lifetime.

Sunday after Sunday, Hanna Marie was prepared to make the Bible stories real in the lives of her precious, but at times mischievous, students.

Rose's mother answered the door to Hanna Marie's gentle knock. "Hanna Marie, I don't know how you handle all those noisy boys and girls, but Rosy cried when she could not attend last Sunday," she said.

Hanna Marie had just stopped by with a picture of Moses and a copy of the Ten Commandments for Rosy to study. She made a point of always contacting the absentees.

"We are having a memorization contest. I have asked the parson if we can have part in the Sunday evening service when we complete all of our memory work," explained Hanna.

The bare cardboard box walls still annoyed the teacher. She did not dare complain to Mamma, but she did mention it to the Lord a few times.

"Lord, I am so thankful I have a separate room for my class, but you made everything so beautiful, I think you would love it if my room was more attractive. Please show me how I can put feet to my prayers." She hung pretty pictures from old calendars and maps of the Bible land to accompany their stories, but, being a perfectionist, she was compelled to lie awake nights awaiting an inspired answer.

The next time Daddy went to town to get some grain ground, Mamma insisted that Hanna Marie accompany him. She needed crochet thread and a few items that Daddy felt unqualified to select.

"It would be good for you to get away from that rug weaving for an hour or so," Greta encouraged. Being a natural salesperson, Mamma excelled in getting her points across.

On this bright sunny morning Hanna Marie was drinking in the fragrance of God's wonderful day. The horses trotted slowly as if to capture the beauty of the trip. After finding just what Mamma ordered and helping Daddy load the groceries, Hanna decided to walk around town rather than watch Daddy grind the grain.

Her hometown seemed so small after living in the big city. You could not possibly get lost here. Hanna Marie turned off of Main Street after seeing a "sale" sign with an arrow pointing toward the largest house in town. A businessman and his wife had owned the house as long as Hanna Marie could recall. The dear folk did not have children. They worked tirelessly in their dry good store until their health began to fail, and the building was then sold.

The stock that remained was moved to the upper level of the home. Yards and yards of fabric had been collecting dust. In their later years, the owners could not ascend the stairs and almost forgot they even owned them. When they both passed away, a distant cousin drifted in to dispose of the property and give them a proper burial. It was the cousin that had posted the sale signs. He was now seated at a stately desk awaiting the neighbors to relieve him of this burdensome task and the goods withal.

Hanna Marie could not help but notice the dry dishes that had been left on the breakfast table for weeks and

Behind the Mirror

dishtowels on a rack just as Mrs. Jurgens had left them the last time she dried a dish. The kitchen clock was waiting to be wound. A few stray mice were scrounging around for some crumbs.

"Everything you see is for sale. There is more on second floor." The announcement came from the front entrance.

Oh! I must get back to the buggy. I am sure Daddy is ready to go. To be sure, Daddy was just about to untie the team and go looking for Hanna Marie.

"Do we have time to go to that sale?" Hanna asked as she pointed to the sign.

Daddy would stop any place her little heart desired. He was well aware of who it was who once tirelessly cared for his farm home and now tenderly cared for his dear wife.

Hanna Marie had just sold a few of her rugs. "I won't be long Daddy," she stated assuredly.

She was on her way up the winding stairway, as though a magnet was tugging at the very soles of her feet. It was the dream of any seamstress, reams of fabric that inspired visions of dresses, aprons, quilts and curtains. Then going to a dark corner, she discovered an answer to her prayers.

"How much are the rolls of oilcloth?" she hollered down the stairs.

On second thought, she hoped no one heard her. She would need the entire roll of one pattern to cover the walls of her Sunday school room. She rushed down the stairs.

"I am open to any offer," the cousin of the deceased declared.

He was eager to return to his own business. The house was cold and lonely now that he lost his loved ones. "I want to get rid of this stuff," he murmured to himself.

Eli could not believe his eyes when he saw the load Hanna Marie was carrying as she returned to the buggy. At least he assumed it was her behind those rolls and rolls of material.

Verlie Eva Miller

"What in the world are you going to do with all that?"

He was still more in shock when she dropped her load and went back for more. Eli did not want to question his dear daughter's sanity, but today he was perplexed.

Hanna Marie knew in her heart there was no use trying to explain the matter to Eli. The horses trotted home while the twosome sat in silence. Eli was endeavoring to keep peace while his rider was dreaming of sewing up a storm and selling aprons and quilts, and she could not wait to cover those cardboard walls. She found a package of wallpaper paste at the five and dime, and all she needed now was the water to mix it. They dropped off the heavy rolls at the church and hurried on home. Greta had piping-hot potato soup ready.

"I am starved!" Eli made no bones about it.

Hanna Marie may have been hungry, but it was the furthest thing from her mind. She had convinced Eli that they would just leave the rest of the reams of fabric in the bottom of the buggy until she had time to explain herself to Greta.

"This is such good soup, Mamma," Hanna said and she hurriedly ate.

Realizing she was going to need a good deal of energy, Hanna helped herself to seconds. Hanna Marie began to explain the rationale of buying out the store, knowing that Mamma of all people knew the value of a good bargain.

She carefully began her introduction. "Oh, Mamma, you would have had a hay day with me today." She painted a perfect verbal picture of the entire scene, every detail. Greta could visualize the thick carpet leading up the winding stairway. She felt herself wanting to grab the dirty dishtowel and broom to sweep down the cobwebs.

Hanna Marie finally disclosed the heavenly surprise on the second floor. Greta was allowing herself to get into the story. "He was open to offers, and I used all the money from the two rugs I sold for every ream he had. Mamma, it is out in the buggy. I will bring some in for you to see." Mamma questioned this deal until she witnessed the beautiful fabric that Hanna Marie displayed.

"Won't this make a beautiful back to a quilt?" and "I would not mind a dress out of this," were a few of the exclamations flying back and forth between the skilled seamstresses.

Hanna Marie knew now that her big trade made sense even to Mamma. She made plans to sew aprons to sell, for she was constantly trying to pay her own way and not burden her aging parents with her own personal needs.

The following day Hanna Marie left early in the morning with a pail and brush in hand. She did not return until her little room was entirely covered with a beautiful scene. The maps and pictures were back in place. She entered the house tired but happy. "Mamma, look!" Hanna declared. "There was still enough oilcloth left to cover your dining room table."

Mamma just beamed. The old oilcloth had been scrubbed until there was barely a pattern left. She admired the new oilcloth and the work of the designer that must have been inspired by the God of nature.

CHAPTER 7

The Walk That Made Memories

Karl was the delight of his parents. By sharpening every parenting skill, they could keep ahead of the little red head. Before they could believe God had entrusted them with this bundle of energy in their hands, he grew right out of their laps. His mother sewed a few shirts and trousers but was never satisfied that they were suitable for Sunday clothes, so she called on the expert tailor. Whenever Hannah Marie completed a new outfit, she had a difficult time keeping her eyes off Karl as he marched into the church with his proud parents. Of course she was careful not to display her pride.

Hanna Marie was always available to care for Karly. Could this be the reason he was so special, or was it because he reminded her of someone in her past?

When Karl was three years old she ripped her old brown coat apart, washed it, and pressed it. The fabric was well worn, but by turning it, a beautiful topcoat evolved. It was as tailored as any coat worn by a prince. Karl strutted across the kitchen when Hanna brought it for him to model.

"Karly, you are going to have to take that coat off now," said his Mamma. She began to unbutton it as he struggled to run off.

Verlie Eva Miller

"I want Daddy to see me with it on," he implored.

"Your Daddy will not be in for an hour," insisted his mother.

Beads of sweat were running down his rosy cheeks. The kitchen range was in full force. A kettle of pinto beans was simmering on the back of the stove. Homemade noodles were on the evening menu to be added to the soup. Anna was grateful that the chickens were laying more eggs, enough for every recipe in her one and only cookbook.

Without siblings, Karl discovered ways of entertaining himself. He learned early in life that he could stay at Grandma's longer if they could not find his socks and shoes when it was time to leave. It was a big joke at first, but when Anna was in a hurry, the hide and seek game was not fun, though Karly enjoyed it immensely. He hid everything he could get his little hands on: gloves, shoes, socks, and hair brushes. The game graduated into utter frustration.

"I can't go to the store until I brush my hair, Karly!" exclaimed his tired mother.

"Well, I don't have a sister to tease like my friend Johnny," was Karly's answer.

Spring sprung, and Karl ran out like a calf that had been penned up all winter. With a surplus of pep and a wild imagination, it was not difficult to entertain him.

"Karly! Karl, Karl! Where are you?"

Anna could not see hide nor hair of her little boy. Panic set in whenever he was out of sight or calling distance, and on this occasion she called again and again while searching the windbreak on the north side of the house. Following a bark in the distance, she found him out in the cow yard. Shag was on guard duty.

Karly raised his head and placed his forefinger to his lips as a signal for his Mother to hush. He was lying flat on his back watching some eggs hatch. The mother bird was rushing around scolding the intruders as the fourth helpless scrawny bird was pecking his way out of the shell to freedom.

Anna was as fascinated at the miracle of birth, as was her soiled little son. Perspiration was mixed with dead grass and dirt in his grubby clothes and curly red hair. Anna stripped his outer clothes off outside and splashed water over his feet and legs before allowing him entrance into her spotless kitchen.

By suppertime, Karl was itching like crazy. His arms and face were covered with a rash. As soon a Hanna Marie received the call, she relayed it to Greta.

"Well, it is either poison ivy or oak," said Karly's grandmother. As usual, Granny was right. They applied her Finnish remedy meticulously, but it took days for his arms to heal.

Anna and Karly visited the bird's nest often, much to the displeasure of mother killdeer. Karly took note of every change in the baby birds, hardly missing a detail nor a newly grown feather. Mother bird tried every trick in her book to distract him to no avail.

"Mommy! Why don't we have a baby?" implored little Karly. "My friend Mattie just had a baby brother! Can we have one, Mommy? I want one."

It was the first time Anna had to answer such a serious question.

Mommy chose her words carefully. "The doctor told us that perhaps we would never be blessed with another child. That makes us all the more thankful that we have you."

"Where did I come from?" asked this bright-eyed lad.

"God sent you to Mommy and Daddy as a little surprise package," answered his mother.

"I like surprises. Why can't God do that again, Mommy? I want to know," he entreated.

The questions arose repeatedly. Anna and Jussel would

have loved to grant that request. All they could do was encourage him and keep him busy.

Whenever the phone rang, right about the time Grandpa would be waking up from his mid-afternoon nap, Karly could always guess who it was.

"Grandpa wants to go on a hike, Mommy," smiled Karl, hanging up the phone and rushing for his jacket. He often walked down by the lake with Grandpa Eli, his soft, little hand nestled in the calloused, worn hand. Grandpa never fully knew the impact his words of wisdom would have on his dear little companion as they strolled through the nearby woods and rambled along the streams.

The nature walks were food for the soul for both the old man and the lad. Occasionally Eli's mood was subdued. Karly was sensitive to the silence that was interrupted only by the crackling dry leaves and the songs of the forest.

"My friend's baby brother is like you Grandpa. He gets crabby when he is tired and hungry and when he doesn't get his nap. He wears baggy pants too."

Eli walked on in silence, wondering how Karly knew he was weary. "Maybe we should go home and play checkers," Karly suggested. He always had a way of winning if Grandpa was tired. Old softhearted folk have a vulnerable tendency to make strategic mistakes when fatigued. They strolled home at a snail's pace.

"Grandpa you walk slower everyday of your life."

"Well, what is the hurry, son? I've had to hurry for seventy years, and I like to slow down and smell the roses with my grandson," answered Eli, with his signature crooked smile.

"I don't see any roses, Grandpa," said Karly looking up and down the lane.

They walked on in silence for some minutes until Karl remembered something soggy in his pocket. "Gramps, if you get hungry I have a peanut butter and jelly sandwich."

Behind the Mirror

Gramps sat down on an old stump. Though not the least bit hungry, he did not have the heart to reject the lad's kind offer. Karl peppered Grandpa with questions, barely giving him time to swallow.

Gramps did his best to step up his pace on the way home. "I can't believe how fast you are growing, Karl," said Grandpa as he bade his little guy good-bye after losing two rounds of checkers. Karly stretched tall and proud, waving goodbye and dreaming of filling his grandfather's shoes one day.

Hanna was taking measurements for Karl's school clothes. It was just a month before he would be trotting down the school trail again to his second grade classes. It was a country school with all eight grades in one room. Concentration proved difficult when the great outside world was so enchanting. He walked slowly, dreaming along as he swung the half-gallon syrup pail. It contained homemade bread, with his favorite egg salad filling, and a bright red apple from their tree. Two gingersnap cookies were on the very bottom, in hopes that they would be eaten last.

"Karl, are you reading your book?" asked Miss Stevens.

Karl was looking out the window as he listened to every class that was being taught. His teacher could not possibly believe he had his reading assignment completed already, but seventh grade science and eighth grade math classes were intriguing, and little Karl did not want to miss the performance.

On returning home, he bid his friends goodbye and rushed toward the house. It must have been the aroma from the pork chops, or energy he expended in soaring through the sky in his own private plane that made him so hungry.

"Mommy, remember what the preacher said last Sunday about feeding the hungry?" he asked. "Well, I am starved for a cookie."

"Supper will be ready as soon as Daddy comes in. We

Verlie Eva Miller

will eat, and then you can have a cookie." She would only have one child, and she was bent on keeping him healthy.

Anna made sure to inspect all pockets before laundering Karl's clothes. One toad floating around in her wash tub was enough. Looking over a wad of paper, she discovered a poem. "Please have Karl memorize this poem before December 11th for the Christmas program."

"Oh, I plum forgot all about that," declared Karl. Anna immediately rehearsed it with him a few times. Two weeks later they were seated in anticipation of the most important part of the program. Hanna Marie appreciated the crisp press in the trousers that she had fashioned. Grandmother regarded the sweater that was knit by her clever hands. Anna and Jussel beamed as Karl recited the poem as though he just finished a speech class. Yes, in labors of love, everyday is payday.

After traipsing through the snowstorms of January, February, and March, spring brought puddles, much to the delight of every red-blooded boy, giving them the thrill of wading until they could feel the water slush inside their boots.

"Karl Thomas" warned his mother, "If you come home with wet trousers and socks tomorrow you are going to go to bed without supper!"

Anna seldom presented such choices to her son. A look of total surprise flashed over his countenance. He secretly prayed that every pond would be frozen over the next day. She just said tomorrow. After all, it was an opportunity to observe the contours of the earth, the temperature of the water, evaporation, and sometimes even little bugs floating. Never has Mother Nature, or any parent for that matter, been able to breed out of the species the attraction of a puddle.

As the years slipped by, Karl did cultivate new interests. The years of leisure were fast disappearing.

"Say, Karl, how would you like to start feeding the calves?" asked his father one morning at breakfast.

"Oh, sure! Daddy, I would like to do that," never thinking of the sacrifice it would mean, crawling out of his warm bed on cold winter mornings. The newness wore off in a hurry.

Soon his father taught him how to teach a newborn calf to drink from a pail. "You hold your hand down in the milk and let the calf suck on your finger until she learns to drink."

Karl did not like that idea. The calf would butt his head against the pail and spatter milk all over Karl's jacket and face. He had to repeat his chores both night and morning. He was now more part of the farm production than he bargained for. He wished for a twin brother or even a tomboy sister to share his chores.

CHAPTER 8

Guardian Angels

There were episodes in Karl's short life that caused Anna to question if he would live to reach adulthood. Once she caught him on top of the barn. He had climbed the ladder Jussel had left propped against the siding before heading to town for some repairs, but it had fallen backward as Karl took his step onto the roof. He yelled until his throat ached, but Anna was in the house with the doors and windows closed. She finally heard him when she came out to hang some laundry. After a fitful struggle she finally muscled the heavy hardwood ladder back into place, just thankful he did not try to jump.

Karl's adventures set Anna praying daily for his

protection. Long chapters could not begin to contain the numerous escapades. Each day was a new adventure. As all parents, they prayed for wisdom, "Lord, how do we discipline this little guy without quenching his lively spirit?" They strove to take his little ambitions seriously, choking back laughter when his ideas were preposterous and yawns when they thought they had heard enough of his ramblings for one day. His were delicate dreams, and Mom and Dad donned kid gloves.

Not one plane that soared the sky above Karl's sheltered world escaped his ears. Every job was postponed until the plane was out of sight. His first book report was on the Wright brothers. The details were so explicit that Miss Stevens began to think he would never quit, and the class was so spellbound that she hardly had the heart to interrupt. The clock over the blackboard was ticking closer to dismissal time, and there were still six more students to go.

"I am sorry Karl, but I have to stop you in the middle of your book report before the brothers ever make it off the ground. That was wonderful," she said, "but lengthy," she chuckled under her breath.

The roar of any motor sent shivers of delight up and down Karl's spine. It was a happy day when Jussel found two old bikes and pieced all the best parts to make one good one. He worked in the woodshed while his son was in school. A fresh coat of shiny red paint with white stripes completed the job just in time for Karl's twelfth birthday.

Karl was elated. It wasn't long before some of Mother's clothespins went missing only to show up clipped to strips of cardboard on the spokes of his bike humming like the sound of an engine. With never a dull moment in the humble farmhouse that sheltered two proud parents and one little fireball, the years vanished like a seasonal blade of grass. If only the walls could talk, the coming generations of occupants

Behind the Mirror

would have had a great deal of entertainment. Anna did take time to record the highlights of Karl's life and her motherly musings in an old notebook, dreaming it could very well be shared with the whole wide world one day.

Karl never missed a single class of Hanna Marie's Sunday School teaching. Dearly loving each student—yet one most particularly—Hanna asked to graduate along with her students each year. After eight years, each student was well versed in the sixty-six Bible books. They could recite every title and quote more Scripture than their parents. Applying them to every day life is what made the neighborhood sit up and take notice, for Hanna's objective was not to merely teach the truth to her students' heads, but rather to reach their hearts, to mold and change them from the inside out.

"Could Karl possibly be graduating from the eighth grade?" Greta asked incredulously, while her nimble fingers darned a sock. Hanna Marie was rolling out biscuits and could not reach for her apron to wipe the tear that was sneaking down the side of her nose. She had now given up on sewing his trousers. Anna ordered overalls from the Sears catalogue, along with chambray material for Auntie to make tailored shirts. At least she was still needed for that.

The whole family loaded in Jussel's car to witness the graduation. Grandpa complained a little as he lifted his knee to get in the car. "I can get in my buggy easier than I can get in this contraption," he muttered under his breath, hoping no one heard him. Grandpa was still proud of his strong team and his shiny carriage.

Sitting straight and tall with his felt hat resting on his knee, Eli beamed as Karl Thomas walked across the platform to claim his diploma. He was glad his thoughts were confined within the heavy head of gray hair. *I don't think there is a smarter boy in this entire state, well at least not in this county,* he assured himself.

Verlie Eva Miller

Grandma and Auntie tried their best to conceal their pride, while the parents beside them gave up and grinned from ear to ear. Grandma knocked her crutches down and stooped to reclaim them. Before doing so, she tipped her glasses and mopped up the salty tears of joy running down her face.

CHAPTER 9

Childhood Left Behind

Life did go on, though Anna yearned for Karl's childhood days to linger. She witnessed her only child growing into manhood before her very eyes. The high school years evaporating into a page of history. Anna had to bite her tongue to drop the letter "y" from Karl's name. Once graduated from eighth grade, Karl no longer answered to "Karly."

"Just call me Karl now, Ma," was this maturing request. "Karly sounds kind of juvenile." When Karl did not respond to Karly, it did not take long for Anna and Jussel to break a habit of fourteen years.

Karl had predetermined that when the time came for him to get serious, he wanted a girl *just like the girl that married*

Verlie Eva Miller

dear 'ol Dad. Though on speaking terms and very polite to all the girls, he was much too busy to entertain the notion of dating. The word did not even fit into his vocabulary.

As Karl increased in stature, his father allowed him to harness the horses, and he was excited to plow, drag, or whatever the season called for. When the corn peeked through, it was then time to get rid of every pesky weed. Riding slowly along behind the horse-drawn cultivator was fun for about four hours at which point the monotony of the cornrows would begin to make him sleepy. He could hear the chug-chug of the neighbors John Deere tractor.

During supper that night, Karl asked the question he had been pondering. "Daddy, can we buy a John Deere?" Daddy shook his head, but Karly pressed his point. "Well, why can't we? The neighbors have tractors."

"Because a tractor can't eat grass, Son." Jussel was extremely conservative. His goal was to soon make the last payment on his eighty acres. Passing the cookies to Karl, he hoped his son would change the subject. Karl, keenly aware of the pressures of making ends meet and of his father's convictions about debt, postponed the tractor subject. It did not prevent Karl from dreaming as he plowed behind Dick and Ned, but he was smart enough to let the matter rest for a season.

The surprise attack on Pearl Harbor was the new and animated conversation over every cup of coffee and family meal. The USA was now joining forces with Europe, not just sending aid to the cause, but flesh and blood.

It was difficult during these days to purchase machinery. Every manufacturing plant was converted to the demands of World War II. The fuselage of the C47 was being riveted as close as St. Cloud, Minnesota.

The crops continued to get planted and harvested each year. It was now Karl's senior year in high school. He plowed and planted on Saturdays, at times grumbling to Dick and Ned, but certainly never with his feet under Mother's table.

Jussel was thrilled to burn the mortgage on the farm that year. This called for a celebration. It was the grandparents and Hanna who were invited to the special dinner. Karl thought the food would be ice cold by the time his father finally concluded his thanks with an, "Amen," which was echoed by every one. The sale of his pigs that year and an increase in his milking herd cushioned his saving account.

If you want to write something that will live forever, sign a mortgage, was a saying that was difficult to erase from his subconscious mind. Jussel gave Anna much credit for the savings. He owed a great deal to his dear wife for her ability to stretch a dollar. Anna canned every edible thing she could get her fingers on. The cellar shelves were lined with canned goods from top to bottom. She could be seen in her garden perpetually weeding, pruning, watering, and tending. Jussel teased that she was as much a permanent garden fixture as the scarecrow he concocted. His dear wife patched and re-patched overalls and socks and created all her own house-dresses. He often held her close and praised her quoting, "Many daughters have done virtuously, but thou, my very own Anna, excellest them all."

Being the frugal pair that they were, Jussel and Anna enjoyed attending auction sales. They did not breathe a word to Karl about the sale bill that Jussel picked up at the bank or the fact that there was a John Deere advertised. He hid the sale bill, just to be safe. Under no circumstances was he going to get Karl's hopes up. Who knows if they would be get the top bid and secure the tractor.

"You are going to take time to go to the auction with me, Anna?" asked her husband.

"I wouldn't miss it," was her quick reply. Days off for Anna were rare. A monthly neighbor club or a weekly trip to the grocery store were the only exceptions. Perhaps she would dash over to the variety store for some thread to match the flour sacks to put the finishing touches on an apron or housedress. Yes, it would be a break in the week and give her more time to spend with her farmer. He may even splurge and buy her a hamburger and a steaming cup of Eight O' Clock coffee from the portable restaurant.

At the auction, Anna was delighted to discover a crock she needed for sauerkraut as well as other kitchen items. She was a bit extravagant when she bid on a beautiful cut glass vase.

"Follow on down," the auctioneer motioned, as they all waded through some long grass to the hill. He did not have to remind them of how well the machinery had been maintained. Neighbors knew it had been carefully sheltered from the wind and the rain, greased and oiled religiously.

The auctioneer finally stepped up to sit on the tractor. "Who will start the bid at $1,000?" Jussel nodded.

Many of the farmers had purchased new machinery before the war. Perhaps they did not have as thrifty of a wife as Jussel boasted of, and just maybe they were still indebted to the banker that was holding the note pad.

"It runs like a top and was never used on Sundays," exclaimed the auctioneer.

George Klemm had owned the tractor only a few short seasons before his only son had been shipped off to a training camp for thirteen weeks and then on to face the invasion of France. George had originally planned to put his machinery in storage until his son returned from war, but, alas, as the story went for so many sad parents in those days, his son would not be coming home. George and Harriet stood in the background as they watched their equipment sell, each gadget, each tool, each machine, and each article. A piece of

Behind the Mirror

their dreams faded with each transaction, and they barely contained their grief.

The auctioneer was seeking higher bids on the tractor. He continued to add the plow and gradually all the equipment was lumped together. Knowing he would need a plow and the basic machinery to go with the tractor, Jussel continued bidding. Just a lift of an eyebrow signaled a bid. Finally to his surprise and Anna's delight, no one else bid against him. The auctioneer earnestly tried to get one more bid, to no avail. "Sold to the gentleman with the wide grin on his face."

Anna wanted to embrace Jussel, but knowing how very modest he was, she repressed the urge and waited until they were in the privacy of their own home. There she would give full sway to her joy. Jussel drove the tractor home with the entire extra bonus trailing it: a plow, the cultivator, a drag, and even a ditch digger.

"It runs like a top," Jussel said to himself as he went parading down the country road. Jussel began to appreciate Karl's love for the purr of a motor. He had the expression of a cat that just opened the bird's cage. The only detriment to his joy was the heart-breaking thought of George's son who was torn from his father's farm and for the parents whose grief he and Anna had tried to console as they left with his equipment.

Anna had sped along with the car in hopes of fixing a special supper for this memorable day, still eager to congratulate Jussel with a great big squeeze.

Jussel reached home just before Karl returned from school that day. His parents watched as Karl came strolling up the driveway, pushing one foot in front of the other with the goal of placing them under the supper table. One look at the machinery that was lined up by the barn, and new life sprang into his feet. He could not believe his eyes. His prayers and dreams were fulfilled and just in time to do fall plowing.

"Karl, you have to come in for supper first!" laughed his mother. The plow was already attached to the tractor and the sound of the motor was music to his ears.

"I am not hungry any more, Ma," he drove off in his dream come true.

Anna knew he was famished; he always was. Jussel suggested he make one round in the field by the house before supper, and he would handle the chores, allowing Karl to plow until dark.

Karl never entertained a dull moment during his high school years. His enthusiasm for sports and his craving for learning preoccupied his mind, leaving little time for the opposite sex. That fact did not deter the girls from thinking, dreaming or talking about this handsome catch, the most popular young man in the school.

The announcement that Karl was chosen as valedictorian created applause and cheers. Karl was a friend to all. His contagious smile could melt an ice cube. It was always his closest buddy that sat with him on the bus until one day when Curt was sick. Heidi seized the moment and plopped into the empty seat, with a slight grin on her face. Now that the longed-for opportunity afforded her, she was speechless. Karl looked up from his book.

"Hi, Heidi."

Heidi managed to get her breath and return the greeting in a soft whisper. She looked over at a group of envious friends. They had spent hours of the past four years on this very subject. How can anyone ever get to sit beside Karl with Curt taking up space?

Heidi was quiet until she realized the only safe subject would be sports. After covering almost every game in the past year, Heidi became a little braver.

Behind the Mirror

"Haven't the past four years flown by?" she asked.

Karl agreed and expressed how he regretted them ending, yet with his zest for life, he could barely wait for tomorrow to dawn.

"Now, I am facing big decisions. I am not sure which college to attend. Guess I do not have to make that decision today," admitted Karl.

The bus stopped at the end of Heidi's long drive way, and Heidi nearly forgot to get off. She ran into her kitchen so thrilled she could barely contain her excitement.

When the bus reached his home, Karl hopped off with a hearty appetite for potatoes and gravy.

"Hey Ma, guess who sat beside me today?" he asked.

Ma could not guess.

"Heidi," he answered. "I couldn't believe how much she has matured in the last few years," he said, his mouth full of a slice of steaming, fresh-baked bread.

"I have been trying to tell you that, and you have been too busy to listen," said Ma with a sly smile.

Curt's phone rang. It was Karl with a special request. "Hey Curt, would you please leave the seat on the bus vacant tomorrow? I am going to see if Heidi will sit with me again. She sat with me this afternoon, and I had never taken time to notice how much she has changed lately. She is really growing into a beautiful girl."

When Karl left with a familiar fragrance of father's aftershave, Anna didn't dare hint of her suspicions. Of all the girls in the Wadena School, Heidi would have been Anna's choice, if she had anything to say about match-making.

Curt gave Karl a wink as he sat down on the opposite seat. Heidi was at the bus stop early. Normally she came running down the dirt driveway out of breath, buttoning her coat. She could not sleep after the exciting bus ride the night before. She secretly hoped Curt would still be sick. It was shocking to find Curt on the bus leaving a vacant seat beside her hero.

Karl had never witnessed such a sparkle in Heidi's eye before. *Where has she been these past four years?* Heidi approached the empty seat as though she were still dreaming. "Is this saved for anyone special?"

"Yes," He answered. "Just for you."

She floated herself down. The twinkle in Karl's eye caused Heidi's heart to jump for joy. The dream of just sitting with him on the bus was fulfilled. *Just for me!* The glorious thought would not escape her for days.

The bus was just braking to pick up Laura. She was well aware that Laura would give her eyeteeth to sit with Karl. Not skipping a beat, Heidi determined to keep the conversation going from where they had left off. Not one past sporting event was overlooked. Karl made a prediction that Wadena would devour Deer Creek in the first basketball game of next season. Heidi could not help but wholeheartedly agree with every word that came from his mouth.

Karl was well aware he would be playing on some college team. *I wonder where I'll be, Minneapolis, Duluth, or St. Cloud?* His thoughts drifted. *Where might this darling Heidi fit into that plan?* He looked her in the eye wondering if she could read those far-off thoughts.

CHAPTER 10

Graduation

"The last week of school and our senior year at that, and finally Karl sits up and notices me," Heidi lamented to Laura in the girls' locker room.

"Well, I wouldn't complain about that for one moment, if I were you, and I wish I were!" she laughed. "Now that you have his attention, who knows what will transpire in the coming weeks. He won't leave for college until fall. You could have a whole summer of fun and romance ahead of you." The girls sat in silence, one with joyous anticipation, the other with a tinge of longing.

It was a switch for Karl to forget about studies, tractors, hunting, and even airplanes long enough to give a girl the time of day. Out of nowhere, Heidi had emerged as a butterfly from a cocoon. Every morning for the five days of school that remained, the most exciting thing for Heidi was to get on the bus, and join Karl on the empty seat reserved just for her.

Graduation day was ushered in by a glorious sunrise with a breeze gently waving both State and National flags. It was with great pride that Jussel and Anna sat on the bleachers and watched their Karl march to the podium to deliver his speech. His friskier, playful, and sometimes ornery days were now a thing of the past.

Grandpa and Grandma sat in chairs that Hanna Marie

had thoughtfully brought with her. That also gave Hanna an excuse to be near the podium. Hanna had been privileged to have that redheaded boy in her Bible class for one hour of each week during eight blessed years of his life. The results were evident in the entire speech. Grandma cupped her tired hand and whispered to Hanna, "We are going to put a copy of this speech along with the dearest treasures we possess in the trunk in the attic."

Hanna Marie never breathed a word to Anna, Jussel, nor anyone, but always in her heart of hearts she wanted to call Karl "Tommy." She relived all the hours she had spent with this now grown-up man. He was still her little, freckled, redheaded boy and *Tommy* was what she silently whispered. She beamed with pride as she recalled the little garments that were products of her nimble fingers. She was grateful that Anna and Jussel had kindly and graciously shared their dearest treasure with her often and willingly.

As Karl continued his speech, the crowd burst into laughter at times and were silent with somber attention as he spoke of the graduating classes that were now in Europe and the South Pacific. This brought to the surface the memories of the graduates from the past few classes that never lived to carry out their dreams for the future. They never were able to be the next generation on the family farm, never permitted to fill the office of the aging family doctor, and all of them were missing important family gatherings, weddings, birthdays, anniversaries and funerals alike. "Their dreams have been shattered by war."

Karl requested a moment of silence. All heads and hearts of farmers and businessmen alike bowed. You could have heard a pin drop, though it fell on a bed of straw. Karl pulled a fresh-ironed handkerchief from his hip pocket while all eyes were closed. With moist eyes and all hats removed the crowd stood to their feet and applauded as Karl returned to his chair. He had spoken from the heart of a young man whose future was still uncertain.

"What preacher wants to follow a speech like that?" the minister asked. The crowd applauded again to show their agreement as well as their eagerness to hear what the minister had to say. Like all good things, the ceremony came to a close. Pictures were taken, short visits had, and then back to face life at home, the blessed center of their world.

Karl's summer was filled to the brim. He had contacted colleges that were on his list, and had received favorable replies. Each college had his record as a star basketball player and put in a bid for him. He would make his final decision very soon.

In the meantime the farm was calling for haymakers, fencers, milkers, and you-name-it. The family managed to keep up with their summer work. Karl pitched in with vigor as he dreamed of the future that was now inclusive of a beautiful girlfriend.

It was midsummer and rain had prevented the harvest of the second crop of alfalfa that had just been freshly cut.

"Why don't you and Curt take the day off and go to the fair?" His father no more then uttered the word and Karl was on the phone.

"Hey Curt, my dad said to take the day off. Why don't you call Laura, and I will try Heidi to see if they will go to the fair with us?"

"It would surely beat mending fences," admitted Curt.

The phone was ringing simultaneously for elated Heidi and Laura.

"What are you going to wear, Laura?" Heidi asked her friend when they had given their beaus their affirmative answers.

There was not much time to dawdle over that decision. Heidi took one last glance in the mirror over the sink and

Verlie Eva Miller

dabbed another coat of lipstick before she heard Karl's footsteps on the porch. Having never dated a girl before, Anna coached him with what a girl expects from a boy.

"Be sure you open the door of the car for her. Pay for her ticket for every ride you take her on. Whatever you do, be sure to have her home by her designated hour. Drive carefully and do have a ..." Before she could complete the list Karl gave her a kiss on the cheek and was on his way to his first real date. *Oh, yes, Karl has been into Dad's aftershave again*, thought Ma, smiling.

"I hope Karl and Curt don't expect to keep those poor girls on machinery hill, or watching some cow give birth, or other masculine interests all day," feared his mother as Karl and Curt drove off together.

"There will be plane rides available, according to the ad I read," Jussel stated. Anna knew exactly what would happen. If there is an airplane on the fair grounds, Karl will be drawn to it like a magnet.

Karl ushered Heidi to the front seat, carefully tucking the corner of her flared skirt just before closing the car door. *Lucky I noticed that*, he thought.

Their next stop was to pick up Laura. Curt knocked at the farm door. Laura's mother came and apologized for Laura. "She should be down in a few minutes. You took her by surprise and she had to wash her hair. Won't you sit down?" she questioned as she pulled out a kitchen chrome chair with a red plastic cushion.

Karl and Heidi did not waste the moments alone. Heidi thought to herself, *take all the time in the world, Laura*.

"Have you decided on college yet, Karl?" she asked.

In truth, Heidi thought Karl had forgotten her entirely the weeks since they had graduated. She only saw him in church, and he always seemed preoccupied or perhaps merely bashful. It was Heidi's first experience of trying to

Behind the Mirror

understand a man, so how was she to discern his thoughts and intentions? Karl was shaking his head in answer to her question, when Heidi came back to the moment.

Laura made an impression on their first date, giving Curt a good taste of what it is like to wait for a woman to get ready. She discovered a forgiving gentleman, whose look seemed to say the wait was worthwhile. Curt, like Karl, was the model boyfriend, opening and closing the car door for Laura. Not quite sure how close to his lovely friend he should sit, Curt observed that Heidi was not exactly going to fall out the door that *she* got in. She had situated herself quite comfortably close to Karl.

It was senior citizens' special day at the fair. The foursome had all been taught to respect their grandparents and elders. However, there were not many senior citizens waiting to ride the Ferris Wheel, Tilt A Whirl, or the Merry Go Round. There were plenty of older neighbors, and the foursome made the mistake of stopping long enough to inquire about Mrs. Munstrom's health.

"I don't think we should ask anyone else how they feel, or we will never get to take our first plane ride." The three agreed with Karl. Mrs. Munstrom had gone into extensive detail about her back pain, sinuses, leg cramps and several additional ailments.

It was decided that the girls and boys would part ways to cover more territory. Laura and Heidi went to see the quilts, the baked goods, jellies, pickles, and needlework. Just smelling and observing the beauty displayed awakened new nesting instincts within the young women. They discussed home decor, kitchen design, favorite sewing machines, curtains, and the best recipe for sugar cookies. They had temporarily erased from their minds the fact that they had been planning a career, and neither Karl nor Curt had ever even hinted a proposal. *This was their first date, for goodness sake.* They chided and laughed at themselves. Just then a breeze with the very taste of a hamburger blew in, and they remembered they were to meet their dates at 12:00 sharp.

"I am so hungry!" exclaimed Heidi.

"You took the words right out of my mouth, and I must not keep Curt waiting a second time today, or he may never date me again."

The guys were there "Johnny on the spot" with a smell of the horse barn overtaking the great aroma of Burma Shave that caused the girls to fairly swoon that morning. They both were as handsome as ever, each in the special way that God had designed them, unpleasant odor, not withstanding. Karl beamed as he looked Heidi over from head to toe, not missing one feature. Not one word had he uttered to give her a clue of his serious attraction, but a gentle reach for her hand spoke volumes, a brave move for a shy guy.

"What would you like to drink Heidi?"

Karl's warm touch dispelled all thirst, though her mouth was dry as cotton. She eventually came to herself and ordered an orange pop.

Curt took good care of his date, and they laughed and chatted together as only schoolmates can, while polishing off the beef and bun.

They finished their fair feast with freshly baked cookies and milk then headed off to buy tickets for the ride of a lifetime. Only two passengers, along with the pilot, were allowed in flight. How thrilling it was to soar over the area and see cars as toys and trees like grass. The fifteen minute ride ended too soon for Heidi and Karl, but when it was Laura's turn, she was somewhat reluctant to go up. She first ran to a phone to call her mother to be sure her parents approved of this big adventure. Curt was impressed that she respected her parents' opinion that highly. They were both happy to once again set their feet back on *terra firma* at the

Behind the Mirror

Wadena County Fair, but Karl wished he could spare another dollar to go again. Heidi would have gone to the moon if that was where Karl longed to be.

Jussel had indicated to Karl that if they decided to stay for the show in the evening, Anna had agreed to help with the chores. It was a good thing he and Curt had saved enough money. Four supper meals were ordered before the show, and every moment was enjoyed to the fullest.

The day ended much too soon for any of the four happy graduates. Curt was sure the bright sunny afternoon had dried out the alfalfa that was waiting to be hauled to the haymow.

Karl strategically took Laura home first. Curt walked Laura to her door.

"Thanks for going with us," Curt said softly.

"I'm so glad you called this morning, Curt. I've had a wonderful time," she beamed.

"Can we get together again soon?"

Laura sparkled under the porch light left on for her and answered, "I hope so!" Then she silently whispered over and over as she slipped off her shoes, *I hope so! Oh, I do indeed. Please Lord allow this to be the first of endless days together.*

Next Karl drove right past Heidi's farm to drop off his best pal.

The car door shut, and Curt was off leaving Karl alone with Heidi at last. He could no longer contain his thoughts for her, though he deferred them at first with small talk, hoping to earn the right to be heard about more serious things. College was a natural subject of conversation. Neither had made concrete plans except to say they definitely knew that they needed to prepare for the future. Final decisions would be made in the coming days.

"Before we say goodbye, I want you to know how much I enjoyed this fun day with you. I am hoping this is just the beginning of our growing friendship. I am sorry I did not spend more time with you during our senior year. I know it will be four years before I can seriously consider settling down, yet may I be bold enough to tell you that I would love to include you in my future plans?"

Heidi was speechless. A tear crept down her cheek. Karl reached for his folded hankie and caught it. He walked her to the house, squeezed her hand as he opened the door for her, and slowly walked away. Not one word in the English language could describe the emotions that Karl and his date were feeling.

Karl decided to go to the University of Minnesota, to the disappointment of several colleges. This provided an excellent excuse to call Heidi, although, no excuse was necessary. She would have been quite content as long as the conversations were mere trifles of sweet nothings. Heidi answered the phone every time it rang, just in case it fulfilled her longings.

Her voice sang with anticipation. She almost added, "Karl" when she said hello before she ever heard a voice.

"Heidi, I have been accepted at the University of Minnesota. What a relief! What did you decide?"

"I plan to go to school in St. Cloud. They have an excellent program for teachers, and my heart's desire is to teach." She paused a moment thinking to herself. *Well, that isn't really my deepest heart's desire.* "Besides, my parents think I will be able to come home more often from St. Cloud."

There was a moment of silence as Karl was hoping they could get better acquainted in the coming months. "Truth be told, I am sure it's best we don't attend the same school. We will get better grades if we aren't tempted to spend too much time together," laughed Karl, endeavoring to think of something positive. They shared how busy they both had been. Karl was rushing to complete some extra farm work, repairing fences, wood cutting, and hauling. The wood would have time to cure, and when the next summer rolled around Karl hoped to be home to help saw the pile in lengths to fit Mom's range and the parlor furnace.

Heidi was sewing her fall wardrobe and helping her Mother with the canning. Karl and Heidi arranged one more date before boarding the same Greyhound bus to school. The distance between Wadena and St. Cloud had never been shorter, and before they could believe it Heidi's destination was announced. There wasn't much time for farewells. They eagerly promised to correspond.

"See you at Christmas, I hope," said Karl as Heidi alighted. The bus driver hurriedly handed over her suitcase; the punctual motor seemed to race restlessly as if to remind the driver to stay on schedule.

Karl had much time to think. The seat remained empty the rest of the journey. Yes, as empty and lonely as Karl felt at this moment. He turned his thoughts to the blessed future.

CHAPTER 11

College Days

Karl was fortunate to have his father's identical twin brother living not far from the University. How could he ever get out of line when it was almost as though his dad was looking right over his shoulder? Years before, Uncle Pekka (now called Peter) had chosen to look beyond the farm to put bread on the table. How very convenient for Karl to have received an offer of a spare room in southeast Minneapolis. Thrown into the bargain were cousins that somewhat compensated for all the years he had longed for siblings.

In quieter moments Karl admittedly missed his mother. He longed to enjoy talking with her as she made his favorite meal, and he even missed teasing her and dodging the wet dishtowel as she would laugh heartily while defending herself against his playful badgering. Of course he missed Heidi more than he would admit to anyone. Between his classes, assignments, and sports, he always made time to write. Letters were signed, sealed, stamped with six-cent postage, and sent on their way to St. Cloud with love.

He promised dear Auntie Hanna he would keep his room tidy, do his own wash, and put up his own lunches. With the modest rent they charged him to inhabit their home, he felt the least he could do was carry a share of the load.

The freshman year was spent covering the basic subjects. Unlike many of his schoolmates, his goal was set. That plane ride at the fair was the deciding factor. To be a commercial pilot was his greatest dream. Not far behind was a wife to share his joys and disappointments. College girls put forth special effort to attract his attention to no avail, for none could distract him or dampen his dream of having Heidi by his side.

Karl did not get home for Thanksgiving. Residing with his close-knit family in the big city, he prudently decided to celebrate Thanksgiving in Minneapolis and save his money for Christmas. For the first time in his life he would buy a gift for a girl with the help of his teenage cousin Kate.

Never a dull moment, the weeks between Thanksgiving and Christmas flew by, and it was soon time to board a bus home for the holidays. It was conveniently prearranged to ride the same bus as Heidi. Typical as it is on a December day in good old Minnesota, snow started coming down in giant flakes. Out on the open roads the wind blew. The trusty driver adjusted his wipers and glanced through his rear view mirror to check to see if he had any anxious passengers.

Because of the holiday season and a shortage of cars during the war, the bus was nearly filled to capacity before it reached St. Cloud. Karl ended up in the very back of the bus, saving as much space as possible for Heidi. She stepped on the bus scanning every seat before seeing a beckoning hand in the rear. Karl slid over to make more room, but not too much, for the new passenger. A crowded bus had never been so convenient, nor so cozy. The sparks fairly flew. Causal greetings were exchanged until all eyes, except for Karl and Heidi's, were on the road conditions. Karl could wait no longer to deposit a first kiss on the cheek of that stunning, flawless face, and the storm was not the subject of the long dialogue. So much catching up and a few sweet nothings slipped out. The remainder of the trip was over, but not the storm. It was a white Christmas, and a joyous one indeed.

CHAPTER 12

Heavy Decisions

Two years of college were now history. Every moment of the summer that Karl and Heidi could spare was spent together, solidifying their love for each other. Many of Karl's schoolmates were now enlisting or called into the service. Karl was constantly weighing the decision to join them. He talked it over with his parents, laboring over the subject. How Jussel and Anna wrestled with the very thought of their only son leaving for the military.

Cautiously recounting the advantages, Karl pressed his point, "Think of it this way, Dad; if I enlisted in the Air

Force, I could get the education and instruction I would need to be a commercial pilot. Who knows, the war may be over by the time I complete my training." Karl felt compelled to enlist, his conscience dictating his duty.

Anna excused herself and escaped to the bedroom to shed a few tears. Karl and Jussel continued the long debate. "Well, Son, I admire your convictions, and I want you to know you have my blessing on any decision you make. Your mother and I will miss you, but we must be willing to sacrifice as well as you."

Karl knew he should tell Heidi in person. He had tried to prepare her for the news; Heidi had read it between the lines of his letters from college, and it was hashed over on every date. It was no secret that Heidi was known to change the subject. Now the moment of truth had arrived. Heidi had endeavored to prepare herself for this announcement, and met it head on, head on his shoulder, that is. She cried her heart out.

"We still have a month to enjoy each other," Karl attempted consolation. "As difficult as it is, we aren't the only two in love that must be separated."

Life did go on. The day of parting was as sad as any day in the lives of all. Farewell parties did not take the edge off of the heart of the matter. There was not much sweetness to speak of in the parting for anyone. Karl was not fully aware of the heartache that Grandpa and Grandma or Auntie Hanna Marie experienced. Saying goodbye to Karl was one of the hardest days in Hanna's life, second only to one dark day in her past to which only a few were privy.

Jussel and Anna were strangely grateful for the months of separation when Karl was in college, for it prepared them for the goodbyes and cushioned the pain of his absence during the war.

Karl was sent to Clemson College after passing an Army aviation test. His basic training was military courtesy, discipline, and learning how to care for weapons and equipment. A five week preflight course was next, then on to a primary flying school for training behind the controls, six months in basic flying, and six months in advanced training with a B-17. Karl knew this was no picnic. He was well aware of what he was getting into. There was a keen sense of urgency to secure more pilots on duty in Europe.

Karl never missed the news of the war on both fronts, hoping against hope that he would hear of surrender. Between 1941 and 1944 the forces grew from three hundred pilots and twelve thousand planes in 1941, to peak strength of 2,400,000 pilots and 80,000 planes by the year 1944. Sadly, 22,900 planes were lost, at least half of them on combat missions. Many pilots and crew members were now prisoners or in their grave.

War is cruel and real, and here I am about to play a part in this gruesome operation. These were the thoughts that accompanied him as he lay sleepless in his bunk.

Letters were his one source of comfort. His letters home were cheerful, for he was still on sacred soil.

> *My Dear Grandparents:*
> *You could never guess how much I miss you both. Granny, I especially miss the smell of your fresh bread and rice pudding. Memories of going on a stroll along the lake with Grandpa always refresh my soul. It brings to mind some of the values Grandpa instilled in my life. I want to say thank you to both of you everyday.*
>
> *And to My Dear Aunt Hanna:*
> *I include special greetings and tell you how many times the lessons I learned in your Bible Classes surface and guide my life today.*

> *I am enjoying the Bible you gave me when I graduated from eighth grade. The days are full to the brim, but never complete without a chapter from the Book you have taught me to love. If ever I need God's protecting hand and guidance it will be in the coming months. I will be leaving for overseas in the very near future. I do not want you to worry about me. Just pray daily for divine protection. My destination and day for departure is a mystery that will be made known soon....*

With care and in lengthy detail, he crafted his correspondence to his loved ones. He wrote countless letters to Heidi, his mom and dad, Hanna Marie and his beloved grandparents, always with the buried, burdened thought that this could be his final letter. *If so, I must share my truest heart so they will never forget how much they mean to me.*

Karl would like to forget the next chapter of his war experiences, though they deserve to be told. Losing his closest buddies on foreign soil was too painful for him to write about. Returning from his last mission, he was met with cheers. The good news came on June 6, 1945. Karl was in no way motivated to reach a goal of thirty-five missions. He did not need to hear the famous "Bombs Away." The war in Europe was now history, except for the clean up. Karl was being sent back home for a month of furlough and then on to the South Pacific.

The storm clouds lifted as Karl was served this notice. He began to dream of seeing his loved ones again. He had time to readjust and process his plans once his assignment was completed. While taking the Greyhound bus home from Minneapolis, Karl was reminded of the trip home for Christmas in the back seat of perhaps that very bus. It was no

Behind the Mirror

less crowded this day, filled with service men, mothers with crying babies, and worn travelers. He felt great respect from everyone he rubbed shoulders with. Who would not respect that handsome man in uniform?

The moment arrived; the bus roared into Wadena. All of Karl's family was waiting. Heidi was in the background, patiently taking a back seat while he greeted his family. After all, she was not family...yet. The grandparents could not hold back the tears of joy. Grandma kept repeating, "Jumala on niin hyvä!" a phrase Karl had heard her say countless times, but now with tears of joy. "Yes, Grandma. God is so good," Karl agreed. Hanna Marie also waited her turn to embrace her dear redheaded boy. She had to stand on her tiptoes to plant her kiss on his grown-up face.

Heidi had the surprise of a lifetime. Their first moments alone, Karl proposed. He found the perfect ring before boarding the ship to return home. Without hesitation Heidi said, "Yes!" What followed were questions that Karl could not answer. "How long will our engagement last?" He knew his next mission would perhaps take him to Japan.

What a cozy sensation it was to crawl into his very own bed. He had dreamed and daydreamed about it for months. No "Nicene" steel huts. No cold cement floors. It was not his turn to gather the wood and light the fire in the potbellied stove. He need not fear that his name was posted for a mission at midnight. He would not be scheduled to fly in the morning. He literally hugged the quilt that Aunt Hanna had pieced for him, and wept like a child.

The day for good-byes descended upon them as a storm in the night. The boy who loved the sound of motors no longer had a sense of appreciation for the roar of the Greyhound bus. He no longer liked the sound of a B-17 or the B-24. He much preferred the sound of his first bike, with Mom's clothespin and a piece of cardboard.

Verlie Eva Miller

Karl saw more of the world than he bargained for. He was sent to the South Pacific where more replacement planes were needed. His deep faith in God and the prayers of his loved ones back home gave him renewed strength for each battle. After the bombings and fall of Japan, Karl was again sent home with discharge papers in his hand. While Heidi was waiting for his return, she had time to plan every detail of their long-awaited nuptials. A beautiful, joyous wedding was soon a reality.

CHAPTER 13

Lonely Days

Years past, bringing inevitable changes including the death of Hanna's dear parents. How very lonely it was without Mamma, and now that Daddy had joined her in the church cemetery, life seemed unbearable.

As she walked slowly to their gravesides, she recalled how God had used past experiences to cushion the blow of death. Next to Mamma and Daddy, Duffy had been Hanna's closest companion, daily following her to the clothesline, chasing rabbits in the garden while she was weeding, and sleeping in a basket at the foot of her bed. Year by year they grew older together. After finding Duffy lifeless one afternoon by the water pump, Hanna's heart was broken. His food and water dishes were carefully packed with his chew toys and mournfully carried to the attic. She decided then and there that Mamma and Daddy deserved her undivided attention and care, and besides, no dog would ever fill his basket.

Her thoughts then returned to the present where she was now facing a season of adjustments. She entered the church and fell on her knees with gratitude to God for his sustaining care. Yet she did have questions, she had many about Heaven but was satisfied that Jesus was saving some things as a surprise.

I wonder if Eli is having a reunion with his first born son? Lord, help me to be grateful that Mamma and Daddy are celebrating their reunion with Papa, and please give me courage to go on.

A new sense of peace filled her soul as she walked back to the graveyard. Once again Mamma was close to her beloved, beneath the grass-covered resting place of Papa. She paused to recall Mamma's last words: "Hanna Marie you have been such a cherished daughter. I believe that God has something special for you. I don't know what I would have done without you, sweetheart, and I have thanked God everyday for your tender care. Jumala on niin hyvä!"

"Yes indeed, Mamma, God is so good. Still, I miss you more than words can convey," she spoke softly to the sunset as she dropped a wild yellow daffodil on the fresh smelling earth.

Mama had died of a heart attack. Daddy was so lonely after Mamma's death that he joined her only two weeks later. His heart had been strong but now it had broken. Hanna Marie had often longed for a quiet moment while caring for her aged parents, yet now those quiet moments had been forced upon her all too abruptly.

She had traveled the path from the church at top speed

many times, but no rush today. No meals to prepare, no wheel chair to push. No cup of cold water to fetch, no bed pans to empty.

Lord, I would be happy to do it all again. Thank you, dear Father, for seeing me through these last few, painful weeks.

Breaking into a run, her graying hair flowing back, she demonstrated her determination to keep pressing along life's path. She arrived home, hungry for the first time in days, only to find, of all things a filthy, stray dog on her back porch. "Well, you poor little orphan! I'm an orphan now, too!" she smiled as she picked him up, and cuddled him close over her shoulder, not caring in the least that her dress would be soiled.

Hanna hurried to the attic to find the dusty dog dishes and brush. Before she would attempt to locate the puppy's master, she bathed her new little friend tenderly and brushed her snarled coat. The dog whimpered as if to say thank you, seeming to love the attention.

"You look as though you could be Duffy's twin. If I don't find your owner you shall be christened Buffy," announced Hanna. After two weeks and no answer to the lost and found advertisements she posted in the paper and around the town, Hanna and Buffy had bonded. Hanna thanked God for this frisky little life in the farmhouse. Buffy was at her new mistress' heels just as Duffy had been, at the clothesline, in the garden, and down to the cellar.

Carrying the wheel chair to the attic was the heaviest load Hanna Marie had ever lifted, but her heart outweighed the chair. How thankful she was that Papa had built a stairway to the attic. Siblings came to pack the clothes and divide the quilts that Mamma had stitched. The shoes that Mamma had worn last and Daddy's old straw hat were the most difficult to pack. They were placed near Mamma's wedding dress in the attic. Hanna's sisters stood silently as the yellowing sheet was lifted. They silently recalled the stories of the wedding day. Not one word was uttered. It was as if they were all tuned to the same channel. Wiping away the tears, they descended the worn stairs.

"Hanna Marie, here is the deed for the homestead. It was decided unanimously that you should have this. Thank you for the years you cared for Mamma and Daddy," her siblings announced.

Weeks passed before Hanna Marie could get her bearings and establish a new routine. She had time to endeavor to set new goals, the dreams that had never been fulfilled. She knelt often by her bedside at sunrise and evening and knew that she was never alone. *Dear Lord, help me to live today and not worry about tomorrow.* "Sufficient unto the day is the evil thereof." This verse from her Bible took on new meaning. *I have enough problems today, Lord. Help me not to borrow from tomorrow.* She crawled into her lonely bed and fell into a peaceful sleep.

Every day, Hanna Marie buried herself in organizing the old farmhouse. Everywhere she looked she saw Papa and Mamma's trail of handiwork. The crocheted doilies on the furniture and the wall hangings drew their artist close to Hanna's mind. She knew in her heart that Mamma would want her to give her belongings to the needy, and it was somehow less painful to have the closets bare.

Hanna rediscovered a talent that she had forgotten existed. "What can I do with Papa's old worn and faded chair?" she wondered. Being a skilled seamstress, a thought entered her mind. *I will reupholster it.*

Hanna Marie delighted in a challenge. She ripped the material off to use as a pattern and searched the Sears catalogue for the just the perfect fabric. While waiting for the package to arrive, the woodwork trim was sanded and refinished.

Behind the Mirror

"Oh, Papa! I hope you can appreciate a finished product," she breathed, gazing heavenward as she carried the completed rocker from the porch back to its respective corner. Hanna Marie pictured Papa in his newly covered chair.

While the days slipped into weeks, Hanna visited the home of each of her siblings. She never missed a day of walking over to Jussel and Anna's when she was home. She missed seeing Karl, but was comforted that Karl and Heidi had each other. Knowing they were content and happy in their own little nest, though many miles away on the West coast, gave the Auntie peace. As always, she came home with a deep desire to have someone to share her life.

Her favorite walk for the day was to the mailbox. If nothing else, the *Fergus Falls Journal* kept her in touch with the outside world. Often there was a letter from one of her sisters to brighten her day. To her surprise a letter arrived with unfamiliar handwriting. *Where have I heard that name?* She wondered. She walked halfway home, spying a stump to sit on. She ripped open the letter in deep wonder and began reading with growing excitement.

> *April 29, 1952*
> *Dear Hanna Marie,*
>
> *I know you will be shocked to hear from me. I trust this letter reaches you. I worked with you for a year or two about 1922-23. I always admired you, and secretly felt much more than that.*
>
> *I was rather timid at that age and never expressed my thoughts for you. I really did not know how much I cared for you until you did not show up for work. So, I sent you several letters. First, I addressed them to your apartment on the third floor. The letters were*

all returned, to my dismay. It was much easier to express myself in writing. A few days ago, I ran into a mutual friend from the company we worked for all those many years ago. She gave me your address. I cannot believe this was all happenstance. Somehow I think God had His hands in this encounter.

A few years after you left your job, I met a young woman that reminded me of you. We fell in love, and had many great years together, until a year ago. She is now with the Lord. For the last two months, I have been thinking of you. The house is so empty and cold. I finally decided I must at least try to find you. Of course I no longer am the "handsome young Italian" that I am praying you remember. My hair is dapple gray, but my eyes are still brown. I heard you remark to one of your working partners one day that you liked brown eyes.

Well, I will not go into more detail at this time. I am sending this to the last name I know for you, as I do not know with certainty if you married, or have also lost your life partner. When you get lonely, you risk at least asking.

Please, would you answer this letter? If our friend was mistaken and you are happily married, please pardon the intrusion. Send me a brief note, and I will endeavor to forget I ever wrote this letter.

I do not dare sign with the affection I could honestly cultivate. I can only state that I am
Sincerely yours,
Ted Palarmore

Hanna Marie sat on the stump in awe. How often her thoughts had drifted in his direction through the years, but she always reigned them in, chastising herself, a mere foolish old maid. While working with him, she had never given a hint of the attraction she had felt for him. When his memory flashed before her, she prayed. *Lord, take these silly thoughts from my brain.* The Lord had granted her request. Now in the quietness of her life alone, the same thoughts surfaced, and she repeated the prayer.

Oh dear me! How long have I sat here? I am absolutely stiff sitting in this position so long. Her dress was damp from the tall grass and moldy stump, but her heart was stirred beyond her wildest dreams. Arriving at home, out of breath, forgetting she was hungry and thirsty, she ran to the desk and searched for the lined tablet and began to write.

> *Dear Ted,*
>
> *You cannot believe how surprised I was to open a letter from you. I have never really forgotten you. In my memory, you were always an outstanding individual. I am very sorry to hear of the death of your wife. I can relate to sorrow, having just lost both my beloved mother and step-father.*
>
> *Allow me to first answer your questions. I have never married. These past years I have been privileged to care for my aging parents. They are now in Heaven, leaving an empty space in this old farmhouse that I love so dearly. I appreciate your effort in locating me. It is always refreshing to renew old friendships. I will be happy to answer future letters and will enjoy keeping in touch with you.*

> *Yes, we all change. You would perhaps not recognize me if we met on the street. My eyes are still blue, but my dark hair, still curly, is now mixed with strands of gray. I admit I am becoming more antique everyday. When I get the courage, I will send a picture.*
>
> *My brother is going into Sebeka this afternoon. I will take this letter to him to mail. How do you like that for fast service? Perhaps we will meet again someday. I never get to the big cities.*
>
> *Sincerely, with thanks,
Hanna Marie*

Ted busied himself by cleaning the yard, painting the fence, and trimming the dead branches out of the lilac and snowball bushes. He always put off going to the kitchen until he was famished. The absence of his dear Lilly, and the want of the aroma of a home cooked meal were unbearable. He searched the smelly refrigerator for palatable edibles. *I must clean this thing before I go shopping.*

His hearty appetite went down the drain after losing Lilly. His pants hung loosely on his hips. Ted tried to find some good music on the radio, in hopes of dispelling his darkness. He twisted the dial until a familiar tune carried him back to Lilly at the piano, his bass voice blending in as Lilly sang "You'll never Walk Alone."

He could hear Lill's voice ringing, "When you walk through a storm, hold your head up high..." The words of the song struck a chord in Ted's being. "Walk on through the wind." *You will never walk alone, Ted. Something good is going to happen to you.* He could almost hear Lilly's voice speaking these encouraging words to his soul.

Even the eggs and toast tasted better now. He poured his

warmed-over coffee in one of Lill's favorite china cups and hummed along with another old song, "Blessed Assurance." Reaching in the cookie jar, there were still a few cookies, which a kind widow bestowed upon him. Suspicious of her motives, he always thanked her, but made sure he did not admit how good they really were. He was not interested in anyone. Or was he? Why did Hanna Marie keep appearing in his thoughts?

Back to the porch with the Minneapolis *Tribune*, he took renewed interest in what was going on in the rest of the world. Glancing up after reading the front page, he heard the mailman coming up the walk. He could not believe his eyes when he nervously sorted the ads from the bills and letters to find one, addressed in feminine script from Sebeka, Minnesota. His hands fairly shook as he opened the letter. He read it over and over as he sat in the porch swing. Hanna Marie is still alive and *single*. *Forgive me Lill, no one could ever rob me of our precious days together, but I am so lost without you.*

Picking up the paper that had blown across the porch, he went directly to his desk and poured out his heart.

CHAPTER 14

The Mail Box

Hanna Marie did her best to erase romantic thoughts but failed miserably. Still she continued on with redecorating the farm home, often wondering how it would look if Ted himself adorned the place. With the energy of a twenty year old, she worked tirelessly, always doing just one more task before calling it a day. Mamma would be so proud of the sparkling windows and the perfectly ironed curtains, and the freshly painted rooms. These improvements were refreshing to Hanna's soul, and brought new hope for the future.

The walk to the mailbox was the highlight of each day,

and it was not just to read the funnies in the *Fergus Falls Journal*. It had been four trips to the mailbox since the arrival of Ted's first treasured letter.

The mailman was impressed at always find her waiting. "Good morning, Hanna Marie. Fancy you having time to meet me each day."

"Yes, with no patients to care for, the days are long," admitted Hanna.

With that she almost grabbed the mail from his extended hand. She wasted no time in further dialogue. Ted's handwriting stood out boldly among the insignificant mail. Breaking into a run when the postman's car was out of sight, she entered the farmhouse fairly panting.

Tearing open the letter, with heart pounding, she read in silence.

> *My Dear Hanna Marie,*
>
> *Words cannot express my gratitude for your quick response to my letter. I now feel more free to write my deep thoughts to you. May I be so bold to admit it? I am so glad you are single. I have no idea if you could learn to love me, or if you would even consider getting to know me, but I would like to extend the invitation. During my happy marriage and all the years of raising a family, I thought of you only if I looked back at old pictures. I once told Lill that she reminded me of a girl I worked with. That would have been you.*
>
> *Lill and I had three children. Our oldest son, Scott, lives in Texas. We have a daughter that lives in St. Paul. One sweet son was taken from us shortly after his birth. I am comforted that Lill is with him now.*

I won't tell you my whole life history, or we won't have anything to talk about when I come to visit you. Suffice it to say that I had a wonderful life until I was left alone, prematurely. If you would like to come to Minneapolis I will be happy to meet you wherever it is convenient. I would also be pleased to visit your farm. I do miss the farm that I grew up on. In other words, you do not need to read between the lines to know that I am excited with just the thought of seeing you again.

Hoping for an affirmative reply by return mail.

Your old admirer,
Ted

Hanna Marie could contain her secret. No, not another minute. *I must just tell someone.* Two longs and a short on the old wall-phone were all it took to have her bosom confidante, Anna, on the other end of the line. "Oh, Anna! You will not believe who I had a second letter from today!"

"I can't begin to guess," said the baffled Anna.

"An old friend that I worked with years ago." She continued on, "He wants to renew our friendship. I will be over to tell you more as soon as I have a bite of dinner and finish a few things that I must do."

Anna met Hanna Marie at the door with a big hug. "I have been praying for a friend for you, and this is the answer." Two cups of tea later, Hanna left with a light heart, having shared her secret dreams and fears with her dearest friend.

Meanwhile, Ted stirred up the courage to call his daughter Ruth. "Ruthie, I think I am finally ready to allow you to clean Mom's closet. I just couldn't bear it until now, but I have decided that holding onto her clothes does not bring her back. I would like some needy soul to make use of them. For months I just loved to smell the sweet fragrance of her dresses. It has all but vanished now. I must go on and face the truth."

"Daddy, I was hoping you would make this decision soon. I have a neighbor who is just Mom's size, down to her shoes. She has been such a comfort to me this past year and is always sharing with others. Mom took such care of her clothes, and they will be a welcomed gift for my friend. I will be over tomorrow."

Ted continued to busy himself with cleaning the kitchen woodwork and cupboards. Finding Lill's failed prescriptions was most discouraging. Turning his mind to mail time gave him new hope. He counted the days since he sent his last letter. The fifth day he met the mailman with great anticipation. Shuffling through the mail, he tossed almost all aside and opened the awaited letter.

> *Dear Ted,*
>
> *I must be honest with you and tell you how delighted I was to hear from you so soon. I am not sure if it is because I am so lonely or if I have allowed feelings from the past to surface.*
>
> *Rather than wonder at what might have been (had we both not been so timid) we can simply rest assured that things happened as God destined. It is so good to know that you enjoyed your years of marriage to your beloved Lilly. Singleness seems to have been my calling these past years, needed as I was to care for my parents.*
>
> *I am I eager to see those brown eyes again and time has undoubtedly made improvements. Since I do not drive much, a visit in the country*

would be preferable. I only learned to drive when my stepfather could no longer handle the wheel. My own Papa would never allow girls to even drive a team and buggy.

You may completely change your mind when you see me, making this first trip your last. I must admit that I am not the beanpole I was at twenty-three. So, no great expectations! I am taking the liberty to plan dinner for you on May 2, if you would like to come to visit. My brother Jussel who lives a mere half mile from my farm will provide lodging for you. It would be a long day for you to return to the city in one day.

I am enclosing directions to the farm, forgoing the temptation to include a photograph. I am not going to risk scaring you away. I will be at church until about twelve fifteen. If you arrive before eleven you will be most welcome to attend the service. It may stir a bit of conversation. We need a new topic in our country gossip column. Looking forward to your visit.

Your <u>old</u> friend,
Hanna Marie

Ted was exuberant. He, like Hanna, just had to share with someone. *Lord, I do not want to rush into anything outside of your will, yet I feel your approval of this. I will continue to pursue her, Lord, trusting you to block the path if I misstep out of your best plan. Prepare my children should the plans you have for us progress. Amen.*

With that he surprised Ruth with two calls in one day. "Hello Ruthie, I just want to share what I feel is good news and get your feedback before I go over the brink. I never thought it proper to tell you this, but long before I met Mother I was attracted to a young woman named Hanna that was very much like your dear mom. Of course, when I met Mom, Hanna completely slipped my mind, but recently in my lonely hours, my mind has wandered back to her. The surprising way we rediscovered one another encourages me that it could be part of God's plan. Before I pursue this any further I want to have your blessing."

"Oh, Daddy!" said Ruth finally able to get a word in, "I would be so happy if you could share your life with someone. I know how closely you walk with the Lord, and I'm going to trust your judgment and heart. I can't wait to share this with Scott. On second thought, I think you should tell him."

Ruthie kept her word and was knocking on the door early the next day. Her arms were loaded with containers to pack the clothes. She wanted to get at her assignment before Dad changed his mind. Ruth had prepared her heart for the possibility of this day. "Dad, do you think you should be here while I remove Mom's belongings? I know how difficult this is for you."

"No, my dear, I must be strong. I have prayed for courage, and God has given me complete peace. I know Mother would be pleased to have your neighbor make use of her clothing. It's important to me that I am here with you today," he said, his soft eyes misting a little.

With that, he led the way to Lill's closet. A faint fragrance of her favorite perfume penetrated Ted's nostrils. He took a deep breath then reached for the dress she wore on their thirtieth anniversary. He stood in silence, and Ruth did not interrupt that sacred moment. She paused a while and then placing her head on Daddy's shoulder; they both released their emotions.

"There, we both needed a good cry," Ted said as he patted

Behind the Mirror

her moist shoulder, then he squeezed out a smile, and uttered instructions, "Let's get on with our project."

They packed in silence. Ted put all the shoes in one big box, wiping them tenderly as he handled them. Ruth decided to leave most of the gowns on hangers. The drawers were pulled out and emptied. The bathroom cabinet was soon free of creams, powders, compacts, and every trace of Lill. It was a sober twosome that carried the things to the car.

"Now let's go to Murray's for a bite to eat, as my cupboard is as bare as Mother Hubbard's," confessed Ted.

Ruth admired how clean the kitchen was, with the exception of the refrigerator. "We have time to clean this before we go eat."

Ted was happy to comply. He had procrastinated that job for days.

"Dad, how do you feel now?"

"Hungry and at peace with what we accomplished."

They ordered an old fashioned dinner. Ted announced that he was making a little trip up to northern Minnesota. Ruth was not surprised. Ted reached in his pocket and shared the creased letters with Ruth. A big smile crept across her face as she read them. It did not go unnoticed by Ted. Stopping at the store was a necessity, Ruth insisted.

"Dad, you are out of eggs, milk, and even bread."

"Well, I don't want to buy too much; I am leaving tomorrow morning. I decided to stay one night, most likely returning home on Sunday. It'll give me a chance to get acquainted with Hanna's brother and his wife." He did not mention the fact that he could barely wait to see his old friend, but he could not hide his feelings from his daughter. She could see it as plain as day.

"Did you make these oatmeal cookies?" Ruth asked, reaching for one.

"No, Lida across the street manages to keep that jar full."

Verlie Eva Miller

Ruth joked at how popular he was with the widows in town. It was the first time she felt comfortable about kidding Daddy. It was then time for Ruthie to prepare dinner for her own family. Theodore and Lillian would soon be home from school, and with that a peck on Daddy's cheek, and she was off with her packed Chevrolet.

That morning Hanna Marie woke up with a joyful heart. The lilacs were blooming and birds singing as Hanna Marie joined in by humming an old song her Mother sang in Finnish. The garden maid put on her gloves and straw hat to rake the yard. Flowers were her first love, but raking leaves must precede the fun. She was determined to have the farmstead looking like a park when Ted arrived. The front yard was as clean as her sitting room carpet and just as green. A growling tummy reminded the little farmer that it must be high noon. "I am so thirsty," she spoke loud and clear as if the birds or Buffy the dog could understand, and for all she knew they did. Today it seemed like anything was possible.

Throwing her hat and gloves on the swing and rushing to the enamel water pail, she dunked the matching dipper and drank at least six ounces. Forgetting how hungry she was, she went for the mail. The flag was down so she knew the mail had arrived. Reaching in the box gave more excitement lately than she had experienced in the past thirty-five years. It reminded her of Christmas.

Just one letter today, that was all she had prayed for. She was going to sit down on the stump to read it. Word had spread through the grapevine that Hanna Marie met the mailman every day and then sat on the stump for hours. She thought she saw curtains move and a shadow from Myrna's front window. Hanna Marie hurried on home. Exhausted and famished, her physical condition had no bearing on what must come first. Tearing the envelope into pieces, she rescued the message and devoured the letter.

Dear Hanna Marie,

Thank you for the lovely invitation. I have decided to leave on Saturday so that I will be able to attend church with you on Sunday. I am not sure I would make it by eleven on Sunday otherwise. Forgive me if I am rushing you. I have told my family about you. Ruth wants to meet you.

If my early arrival does not work for you please call collect at HA2- 2648.

Hanna read on, and the hungry feeling had vanished. *Could one live on love? Could I really, really fall in love with someone I haven't seen in years?* She pondered on this matter while swinging slowly on the creaking, faded swing. She thought how Papa and Mamma enjoyed this very swing when Papa first built it. She could hear them now talking of family and of days in Finland. She found herself thinking in Finnish. "Jumala on niin hyvä!" she rejoiced.

Reading the letter one more time reminded her that she had one less day to prepare to meet Ted. Making a mental list of her baking, cleaning and personal care, she left the swing bobbing in the wind.

Saturday was upon her before she knew it. Every detail planned and timed strategically, she mixed the bread early in the morning to draw it fresh from the oven before Ted's arrival allowing the aroma to linger long enough to welcome him. A big batch of potato salad was in the making, and a lemon pie rested on the pantry shelf. Hanna Marie forgot all about greeting the mailman today. The letter she was waiting for was a living epistle, and her heart's desire would not fit in the box, but rather would arrive a moving, breathing being with a pulse.

CHAPTER 15

The Flowers Bloom

Ted arose on Saturday morning at the break of dawn. Singing in the shower, he nearly scrubbed his skin red. A good cold rinse, and he was wide-awake. "I'll just stop at the diner for pancakes," he murmured to himself. He was in much too big a hurry to tidy up a kitchen. Shaving with Burma Shave and splashing on his favorite after-shave, he packed his personal gear in a small case, loaded it in the trunk, and he was off.

He could not go by the cemetery without stopping to visit Lill's resting place. He paused to thank God for the memories, asked for a safe trip and His blessing. Then pulling a small bottle of Lill's favorite perfume that he had rescued from Ruth's packing, he let droplets fall on the artificial bouquet. *I'll be back on Mother's Day with fresh flowers, Lill.* He stood in silence thinking. It was the first time Ted did not shed a tear while standing by her graveside. He had a long trip ahead of him and throwing a kiss, he walked away soberly. Having had time to think about the past, he now felt the promise of the future.

The chickens in the yard scrambled, and Buffy began barking. Reaching for a clean apron, Hanna looked out the window. It was Ted just closing the door of his car. Walking as straight as a soldier, looking as handsome and confident as ever, he knocked on the front door. Hanna Marie glanced in the mirror over the sink, brushed a few stray curls back, and opened the door. Reaching out her hand, smiling from ear to ear, she managed to say, "Hello! Come in Ted. I am so happy to see you." Hanna Marie reached out to shake his hand, but Ted pulled her close, and his left arm gently folded around her waist. "It is so good to see you, Hanna. You look just like I pictured you in a dream I had last night," he said pulling back to admire her.

"I think we have both, shall I say, matured in the years since we last met," Hanna said laughingly, still stunned from the thrill in her heart. *He hugged me! I haven't been hugged by a man since...*

"I haven't smelled such a wonderful aroma of homemade bread since Lill became sick," he said as they strode into the kitchen. "Oh, please forgive me for referring to her so soon. I promised myself I would not do that."

"That is perfectly proper. You will hear me talking of Papa, Mamma, and all the loved ones I miss. May I take your hat?"

Ted had removed his hat before even thinking of entering the door. He had such respect for the Hanna Marie he remembered. They sat down at the table to enjoy the home cooked meal. Ted called it lunch. The cook considered it dinner. Whatever it was, he was ready for it; the pancakes had worn off long ago.

"This is what I call good cooking!"

Hanna Marie just beamed. "Would you like to walk over to my brother's? It is just a half mile." Then glancing at his spit-shined shoes, she added, "Maybe we should drive, or take the buggy," with her face breaking into a grin. Hanna took him out to the machine shed to see the buggy.

"I just can't part with it. This buggy was in service long after everyone else traveled by car. I can see Daddy and Mamma taking off in the buggy to church or to Sebeka. Mamma would never think of leaving home without her hat and gloves, and Daddy with his Stetson hat. Daddy wasn't extravagant, but I think he would have mortgaged his horse to possess a Stetson."

Before Hanna Marie knew it, she was telling most of the family history, but not quite all the family secrets. Ted could hardly do more than nod or smile. He observed so much about his guide, and taking her hand they strolled around the flower garden. The tulips welcomed their admirers.

"Hanna Marie, you are just what I imagined you to be." He stored many of his thoughts, allowing Hanna to share her life for now. They did drift back to the house for a swing on the back porch until they heard the phone ring. It was Anna, inviting them for supper at five.

Ted ushered Hanna Marie to the car and closed the door gently. It reminded her of Daddy and Mamma. She could just see Daddy assisting Mamma as she climbed in the buggy. Hanna had never experienced such a gentleman. The car was as shiny and spotless as Ted's shoes.

Myrna waved from the garden as the strange car drove past. She did not bend over to pull a weed until both the car and the dust were out of sight. "I could swear that was Hanna Marie in that front seat, but I never saw that man in all my born days. Land sakes." Pushing her straw hat back, she pulled up her apron to wipe her beaded forehead.

Jussel was out in the yard, anxiously waiting to meet Ted. Hanna had to have his approval before she went off the deep end. Ted went around the car to open the car door for Hanna Marie. She felt like a princess for the first time in her life.

"Jussel, I am pleased to introduce you to Ted Palarmore."

Jussel gave him a strong farmer's handshake. Grins spread across two handsome faces. Anna was at the door by this time and introduced herself. Following her in the kitchen, the smell again created a hearty appetite.

"This has been a wonderful meal, Anna," Ted commented again as they finished their last bites. Hanna nodded in agreement.

"Would you two care to seek out the source of the Mississippi?" Knowing it was just a little further north on 71, it was something Ted had always wanted to do. Having lived in Wisconsin, he had never explored northern Minnesota. The trip was planned for Ted's next visit. They would pack a picnic and drive to Itasca for a day of hiking and exploration.

After a long evening of chatting, Hanna suggested it was time for her to get home.

"I promise I will have dinner for you three tomorrow," she said as she dashed out the door to walk home.

"Hanna, you can't walk home alone in the dark," Ted said as he started for the door.

"Don't lose your way back, Ted. We will be up for a while," Anna stated.

Ted saw Hanna to her door, kissed her hand and thanked her for the pleasant day. Hanna could not think of words to express how delightful the day had been.

"Thank you, Ted. We will leave for church at 10:45."

"I'll pick you up," Ted volunteered. The next morning, Anna and Jussel occupied Ted's back seat to the old farmstead. Hanna Marie was in her best summer dress, blue cardigan, and white shoes. She was accustomed to walking to church in her old tennis shoes, carrying her white shoes until she left the gravel road. Ted met her halfway and clutched her arm as though she was incapable of walking alone, then closing the car door they were on their way.

Jussel and Anna led the way into the church and Hanna and Ted followed. The Minister was just getting up from his knees. He stood silently while all eyes were on the stranger that was with Hanna. The singing, formal readings and confessions preceded the sermon of fire and brimstone; the preaching was as if they had a church full of back sliders.

Entering the farm home with the chicken and dumpling aroma reminded Ted of his childhood. Sure enough, there was an apple pie hidden on the pantry shelf. After a scrumptious dinner and timely visit, Jussel and Anna decided to walk home. Ted thanked them for the bed and breakfast, the visit, and the open invitation.

"You should have some time alone to get reacquainted," Jussel winked approvingly at Hanna as they walked out the door and down the well-worn path between their farms.

"Hanna Marie I want you to know how grateful I am for this wonderful renewal of friendship. I don't know about you, but I would like to spend this summer learning to know you better."

Hanna was speechless for a moment and then smiled. "I assure you, Ted, I enjoyed this weekend more than any time in my life."

That statement was all Ted needed to satisfy him. With that, he went for his hat and suit jacket.

"Even though in a sense we are strangers to each other,

I think we can pick up where we left off so many years ago," Ted assured.

Hanna agreed to repay his visit by making a trip to Minneapolis in midsummer. Ted could hardly resist giving Hanna Marie a kiss. He would settle for a hug this first trip. Overwhelmed, a dark cloud came over Hanna's countenance, but Ted was too close to notice. Gazing in a sea of thoughts she wondered, *am I dreaming?* Hanna pinched herself and watched the dust rise until the car became invisible. Buffy, feeling a slight bit neglected, rubbed against her to get some attention.

Ted did come back. His Buick could almost find its way to Hanna's doorstep without a map, a compass, or hardly a driver. The trip to the source of the Mississippi was most delightful. The foursome nearly forgot their age. Going barefoot at this noted spot brought laughter and childhood memories. The picnic was perhaps the best anyone had ever served at this famous tourist attraction.

Hanna Marie and Ted spent weekends together the entire summer. Anna and Jussel looked forward to their weekly guest and learned to love Ted as a brother.

CHAPTER 16

Hanna Goes Traveling

Hanna Marie did keep her promise. She boarded a Greyhound bus in Wadena, and Ted met her in Minneapolis. Spending the weekend with Ruthie and Joe and meeting Ted's grandchildren were highlights.

"I would like to drive to my house before you leave," Ted mentioned.

"I would have been disappointed if I did not see your home."

Hanna was in awe of the furnishings and decorating of the home. The flowers and shrubs were most impressive.

"Soon all these flowers will freeze. I spend a great deal of my time out in the yard. It reminds me how short life is, like a blade of grass."

They were seated on the wicker love seat. It was the

Verlie Eva Miller

perfect time for Ted to speak his heart. "Since we renewed our friendship, we haven't been apart a single weekend." Clasping her hand, he cleared his throat and said, "I trust you know me well enough now for me to ask you, will you spend the rest of your life with me?"

Hanna Marie hesitated a moment. "Ted, I could never think of life without you. You have given me such happiness. Before I marry you, there is something I have never told you," and she began to sob. Every time she attempted to go on, the lump in her throat and tears took her very breath away.

Ted held her close and gently kissed her cheek. Then glancing at his watch he panicked. "It is time to get to the station; unless we leave now, we will barely make it," he said while rushing her to the car.

Hanna Marie was relieved that she did not have time to attempt to tell Ted more. The bus was loading, her suitcase was tagged, and she was off. Ted was left in bewilderment, but it did not change his love for Hanna Marie.

"I do love you, Ted. I will see you this weekend," she almost yelled, breaking a weak smile, not caring if the whole wide world heard her or saw the tears streaming down her face.

Seated beside a grumpy man, she prayed that he would soon be sleeping. Her prayers were answered.

Jussel was "Johnny on the spot" to meet his dear sister. Even though Hanna Marie enjoyed her time with Ted and his family, she was glad to be back in familiar territory.

"Did you enjoy your trip, Sis?"

"It was most delightful."

The passenger had very little to say. Jussel endeavored to keep a dialogue active. "We watered the flowers, as that promised rain just blew over. It's mighty dry, but a great time to put that last alfalfa crop up. I almost forgot to tell you, Myrna went to the hospital with a gall bladder attack."

Behind the Mirror

That news awoke the dreamer. "What? Myrna is sick?" Hanna Marie did not repeat what she was reminded of. Some old neighbor had once stated, "Myrna is too ornery to get sick." Hanna Marie did not agree with him, but somehow it popped into her head. Myrna's life had been changed when she turned her life over to Jesus. *Forgive me, Lord, for even thinking of that. Comfort her this very moment.*

"Jussel, I must tell you, Ted proposed to me before I left."

Jussel and Anna had been wondering if Ted was ever going to get around to that.

"He did?" Jussel tried to sound surprised. Jussel's eyes were glued to the road for a spell, as if deciding what questions to ask as they floated in his brain. Hanna offered no more information, so instead, he changed the subject from engagements to a safer subject.

"Our cows broke out of their fence and ended up in your cornfield. Luckily the dog barked and woke us up before they wrecked your renter's crop."

Hanna Marie was weary, but happy to get back home. Buffy could not contain herself. Knowing it was not a good idea to hop up and ruin her mistress' dress, she tried to contain her excitement with a combination of a whine and bark. She wagged her tail until Hanna Marie expected it to snap off and fly to the ceiling. She did take time to stroke her pet, but Buffy would never understand in canine language the change in moods and attention she was getting. Hanna fed Buffy and checked her flowers before heating a bowl of soup.

"I know what I must do, but I am much too tired to do it tonight," she murmured to herself as she slowly ascended the stairs. Buffy heard that, but she was left in the dark, and settled down in her lonely basket, pondering the changes taking place on her territory. Hanna Marie's bed was the most inviting sight she had seen since Buffy was a pup. She slept like a top, tossing all night. When the clock struck five, she decided to rise and write the letter to Ted that she pondered all night.

Ted would come on Friday evening. She would hand the letter to him in person, for she wanted to catch his expression as he read it.

She tossed several attempts in the wastebasket before sealing the final draft in an envelope. Tucking it in her apron pocket, she prepared breakfast and offered an apology to Buffy.

Why on earth does my Hanna not confide in me? Ted was still bewildered when he arrived. Buffy gave him a hearty welcome. Ted caressed her shiny coat, and Buffy ate it up. The lady of the house came out to meet him. "I missed you so much," Ted spoke what both Buffy and he were thinking. Buffy was just as bewildered as Ted; their darling Hanna had just not been herself these past few days. Hanna Marie was not slow to admit that she had missed him terribly.

When they could let go of each other, a pungent odor from the kitchen made them break into a run. How could she allow the potatoes to boil dry? Ted would have eaten burned squirrel. Conversation was carried on between bites, but the real issues could wait, and Ted had a heavy heart. Ted dried the dishes before the swing beckoned them. Hanna Marie reached in her apron pocket and handed Ted the sealed envelope. "I would break down if I attempted to say this, so I've taken the liberty to give it to you in writing."

Ted opened it slowly and with somber expression read its content. Still holding the note, he drew his promised bride close and whispered, "Has Christ forgiven you, dear?" She nodded.

"So do I. It is in the sea of God's forgetfulness."

He walked to the old kitchen range and lit a match to the

Behind the Mirror

note. "We will never talk about this again unless you want to tell me more. There. Now we can proceed with wedding plans," he picked her up and carried her like a child. "I will carry you and your burdens now." Hanna Marie could feel the load lift from her heart. She burst with affection for Ted.

"Question number one, my dear. Where would you like to live?" Ted said as he alighted her on the love seat.

Hanna answered with the same question.

"Hanna, my dear, I would move to the North Pole if I could spend the rest of my life with you."

"I don't think I would ever feel at home anywhere but right here."

"I have been thinking I would not care to live where I would be constantly reminded of Lill, as much as I loved her. I now want to devote my attention to you." He continued to explain, "I have always loved the country, and it will be great to have Anna and Jussel for neighbors. How about if we settle here on your farm?"

Hanna Marie just beamed.

"I would like to spend a few months in Texas near Scott during winters," continued Ted. "It was difficult for Lill to travel these past years, and I need to spend more time with my grandchildren."

Hanna Marie was elated to think that she would get out of the state of Minnesota for the first time in her life. How many times she had dreamed of traveling.

Good-byes were painful now that the two had pledged their lives to one another.

"We are getting a late start, so we are not going to delay this a minute more than we have to," Ted said as he bid her good-bye.

Ted departed with such a light and relieved heart. To think of a future with Hanna Marie was almost unbelievable. It was difficult not to air his feelings aloud. It was a good thing his vehicle was familiar with the path home. Ted's mind was on decisions that must be made. It was with mixed emotions that he faced the sale of his house. He arrived home weary and hungry, having forgotten to eat the sandwich his lover had packed. A cup of tea complemented the sandwich, and there were more oatmeal cookies. *How would poor Lida take the news?*

"Hello, Ruth! How are you?"

"Oh, Daddy, you are home!"

"Yes, and I have the greatest news! Hanna and I are going to set our wedding date."

She then shouted in Ted's ear as though he was deaf. "I am so happy for you, Daddy!"

The decisions that must be made were brought to surface. The sale of Ruth and Scott's childhood home brought tears to both Ruth and her two children. It weighed heavily on Ted's shoulders, in spite of the promised future with his new love. Ted gathered the papers from the porch that Lida had so carefully placed in a plastic bag, along with the container of peanut butter cookies. Ted was too sleepy to even open the bag or the round tin that was still warm from the fresh cookies. He trudged once more to a bed that seemed lonelier then ever.

The shrill ring of the phone awakened him at daybreak.

"Daddy, I have a thought. Your home is closer to Cliff's job then our home. I will talk to him about selling our house instead of yours."

After careful thought Cliff agreed. Ted would charge her half of the value of the home and give Scott that amount. Ted felt a sense of pride in his family enjoying part of their inheritance while he was around to witness the transaction.

"There is not much room in the farm house for all of these furnishings. I will consult my bride after you two decide what you can use."

Behind the Mirror

Everything seemed to be "working together for good." Ruth's home sold two weeks before the wedding. Scott and his family came home to enjoy a week with Daddy before the house was disrupted. A trailer was then loaded in the garage, ready to head south after the wedding day.

Ruthie prepared family favorite meals and grandchildren's laughter filled the home once more. Scott and Ruth recalled the pranks they played and the joys of childhood memories. With everyone around the piano, music penetrated the very walls. Ted missed the soprano voice of his dear departed one. Little Lillian would now have music lessons and Ted was confident she would be an accomplished pianist and soloist like her Grandmother.

CHAPTER 17

Time to Sew!

Hanna Marie gazed down the road until the shadow of Ted's car disappeared into the horizon. She stooped to pick a rose that was about to lose its beauty, thinking of how much it reminded her of herself. "I almost slipped through life without a snitch of real love," she murmured to herself as she breathed in the sweet fragrance while a petal fell to the ground. Buffy rubbed against her legs as though she understood flower language. It had been a long day, and Hanna was the happiest any maiden could possibly be.

She did not know why, but she found herself on the swing, staring longingly up to the stars and the full moon and worshipping the God of the universe with a heart bursting with gratitude. *Oh, how could I have stayed out here so long?* She shivered as the fall air penetrated her very bones. She knew how many things she had to do. With a cool breeze sneaking over her nine patch quilt she fell into a peaceful slumber, dreaming of a wedding, a young and beautiful bride, a replicate of the wedding she fantasized about as a young girl. It took place in a flower garden, with a handsome groom gently kissing her white glove. She awoke with a pang of hunger, and Buffy was licking her hand.

While feeding the dog, watering flowers, and completing her everyday tasks, Hanna Marie made her wedding plans. Ordering ivory satin from the Sears catalogue was first on her list. She decided to brave it and take Daddy's car to Wadena to find a pattern for her gown. She had managed to pass the driver's test a few months earlier. One would have thought she was taking a trip to the big cities the way she implored divine protection as she plunked herself in the driver's seat. There were all of five cars on Highway 71, but her mind was not entirely on the driving.

She found the perfect pattern, picked up a few groceries at the Red Owl store, and thought it best she buzz on home before the heavy traffic.

"It is strange you have any tail left," Hanna Marie said as she assured Buffy she was really home. "I'm not going anywhere yet, but soon you'll have another master in the house."

Anna was to be her maid of honor, and she had asked Ruth if Lillian would be the flower girl and Theodore the ring bearer. Ted had agreed earlier that Scott and Ruth also be their attendants.

Both Ted and Hanna were busy as they spent their first weekend apart for months. It was almost unbearable. If it were not for the phone and his family and grandchildren around him, Ted would not have survived the separation.

"What are you doing, my love?" he questioned her on the phone.

Behind the Mirror

"I was sitting out on the swing with Buffy. She just clings to me but is doing a poor job of keeping me warm. She surely knows that soon she must share my time and attention. She actually reached for the fabric when I was cutting out my wedding dress. It landed on the floor with a few tooth marks on one corner.

"Oh, I am so excited to start sewing on it! I knew if I started it tonight I would be tempted to sew on Sunday. Just think, two weeks from today is our wedding day. I feel like I am about twenty-two, until I look in the hall mirror which is obligated to tell me the truth. I did lose a few pounds. I guess I'm too busy to eat! I completed Anna and Lillian's dresses this past week, and I just need to hem Lillian's after she tries it on. Well, we better hang up; I am not one to run up a phone bill, ever."

Ted reminded her that he would have spent a lot more on gas, if time had been on his side to make the trip. Little Lillian was waiting patiently for Grandpa to get off the phone. She skipped out to the back yard, clutching Grandpa's hand. The twosome gathered a mixed bouquet. She wanted to place it on Grandma Lilly's grave. The three other grandchildren, plus Ruth, Cliff, Scott, Mary, and Ted stood in silence as Grandma's namesake knelt down and placed the vase near the tombstone. Then joining hands, they sang, "Till We Meet Again."

"May we stop at the Dairy Queen?" Max asked with a positive grin. Grandpa would never let him down. It took carefree children to face hard facts and then go on with life. The days together were bittersweet. Scott and Ruth were aware that the family home would never be quite the same again. The four cousins enjoyed being together and Ted tried to hide how much he missed his awaiting bride.

"I don't think I can lift one more thing," Ted groaned as they shoved the last piece of furniture on the trailer. Both

Verlie Eva Miller

Scott and Ruthie were still on speaking terms after making some difficult decisions. Ruthie did not need living room furniture; Scott had the exact place for it in his new home. Ruthie wanted to keep the dining room exactly as Mom had it. She promised to serve old favorite Sunday dinners every time Scott came to visit. It was with a sigh of relief that the whole gang crawled into the beds that were left intact.

Ted thought he would die before he could face another day like that one. Before he knew it, he would be planning a picket fence and painting all the buildings on a farm in Northern Minnesota. *I wonder how Hanna is coming on her dress?* With that thought he imagined her marching into his arms in a long gown and fell into a deep sleep.

The next day Hanna Marie finished her dress. She bathed, put the entire trousseau on and marched up and down before the hall mirror. Her shoes were the same shoes that Mamma wore at her wedding in Finland. They reached the calf of her leg and buttoned all the way up. The hook to button the shoes was carefully tucked in the shoebox. Once a year Mamma had given them another rub down with special oil. They were as soft as the day she wore them.

Oh, Mamma, I wish you could see me now. She had a very special reason for wearing that style of shoe and Mamma's wide brimmed hat.

A knock on the door startled Hanna Marie. *Who could be coming unannounced?* It took time to unbuckle her shoes and all the little buttons on her gown, and she did not dare be careless with her nylons and gloves. Another knock and another. She was just about dressed when the knocking became louder and louder.

The door had been double locked for the night. Peeking through the window she saw Ted's hat. Ted met her with open arms. "I was just about to leave. I stopped at Jussel and Anna's, and they said you would be home. I could not bear another weekend without you. Were you in bed already?" He took a deep breath and gave his lover time to explain.

"No, Ted, I was not in bed. I completed my gown today and was trying my entire wardrobe on to be sure everything fit. It took a little time to take off the dress and get dressed again, and I was not about to come to the door in a wedding gown! I did not expect such a happy surprise."

"Come, sit on the swing." Ted could contain his secret, not one more second. He held her hand and placed on her finger the most sparkling diamond that Hanna Marie had ever stared at. "I can think of no one I would rather spend the rest of my days with."

Hanna was speechless. She buried her head on his bosom and wept for joy. Darkness invaded the sacred silence, and words were not appropriate.

"Well, now that my home is sold, we must decide what we need for our home."

"I have never been able to even dream of refurnishing a home, but I would love to have a new bedroom set." After much discussion and thought, they made plans to visit a furniture store in Wadena and Brainerd the following day.

Ted arrived early from Anna's the next day.

It was like a dream come true for Hanna Marie. They ordered a bedroom and living room set, a few new lamps and pictures.

"I am hungry, aren't you?"

Hanna agreed that making all those decisions in one day burned up a few calories. The stores would deliver the following day. The old furnishings were carried to the attic one by one but not without a tear or two and a historical story about each piece. The rooms were cleared, except for Papa's chair, and just in time the truck with the furniture was backing up to the front door.

"I simply cannot take Papa's chair to the attic." Hanna

Verlie Eva Miller

Marie said tearfully. Ted tenderly comforted her, agreeing that it was too precious to tuck away. It was beautifully covered now and added a chapter of history. When the furnishings were all in place, they sat together on their new couch and planned their honeymoon. Papa's old rocker seemed to nod in agreement with every plan, and they knew their secrets would be safe.

"We won't go far for a honeymoon now until the harvest of your garden," Ted insisted.

Hanna had a wonderful crop of squash that year. There were apples to pick after the first light frost. Ted was eager to get to work on the picket fence before the ground froze, and he could think of no better place to be, snug and cozy together in the farm house until after Thanksgiving.

Every trifle was worked out from the honeymoon to the ceremony, and some details would come as a total surprise to the guests.

"Oh I must get going before Jussel locks me out." He could hardly believe it was 10:00 p.m.

Hanna Marie sat and drank in the furnishings. She was happy she had painted the walls before all the wonderful surprises God had planned for her. *I must get to bed. Tomorrow I will go to Wadena and buy a set of queen size sheets and a new spread for this gorgeous bedroom set.* With that, she trudged upstairs vowing she would not sleep in that new bed until she had a partner. It was much too large for one person.

The special couple was invited to Myrna's for supper the following day. That was unusual. They arrived just five minutes before the meal was to be served, and Jussel and Anna popped in also.

"You never told me you were also invited," Hanna Marie whispered.

Myrna nearly out did herself. The luscious assortment of vegetables, mashed potatoes, pork roast and apple pie hit the

Behind the Mirror

spot. They covered years of memories, and the dishes were done before they knew it.

"Let's all walk down by the lake and cool off," the hostess suggested.

They talked of the drowning that had occurred in that very lake. Jussel would never forget that. Though often recalled, Ted had never heard the story. Jussel proceeded to tell him. "If you're going to live next to that lake you're going to hear this story. As a living witness, I will tell you. You may hear many versions of it."

The twin brothers walked around the lake to get to the country school until the lake froze, and took the short cut over it. A neighbor boy often joined them. It was March and there were weak spots on the edge of the lake. "I think it is still safe," David assured them as he slid ahead, wishing he had his skates. The snow covering had all but disappeared. "Before our very eyes David was out of sight," Jussel continued. "We started rushing toward him as the ice began to crack and realized we were all in grave danger. We rushed for help but were too late." It was a sobering thought on such a memorable evening.

"There is sure a lot of traffic on this country road for a week night," said Ted, perplexed. Myrna acted like she never heard him. They walked on home, and the yard was full of cars, with others parked on the side of the road. After all the surprise showers Hanna Marie had planned, she was in for one herself.

It was as well thought-through as she would have done herself. Neighbors dressed the entire house with bouquets from choice fall gardens. Opening the generous gifts of linens, glassware, clothespin bags, and the latest gadgets raised grateful comments. Hanna Marie could use some new things. Mamma's old towels, utensils and clothes pins had seen better days and would be carefully stored in the now crowded attic. Ted enjoyed meeting the men that attended and was thrilled to make new friends in his new rural setting.

They loaded the gifts in Jussel's car as well as Ted's. Thanking Myrna for the meal and party, they headed for home. By the time the packages were in the dining room, Ted hurried back to Jussel's, but not before tenderly kissing the hand that boasted a new diamond.

"Just three more days, and we can enjoy being together forever."

Hanna could hardly settle down. It was out of character for her to go to bed with anything out of place. Ted must be included in the unpacking of gifts. After all, they were also his gifts. How could any normal person get to sleep after all that excitement? Sheer exhaustion sent her to the land of nod by the time the clock struck twelve.

CHAPTER 18

The Wedding

The days were filled with unusual busyness. Hanna Marie cleaned every nook and cranny of the house. Families began arriving daily. There would not be room for all the brothers, sisters, nieces and nephews in the old farm home. Anna and Jussel provided housing for several. City nephews had the bright idea of sleeping in the haymow. It was filled with fresh alfalfa hay. The cousins could hardly wait to camp in the barn. The bride volunteered her new bed and gave up her old bed to two of the nieces while she moved down to the new couch. "I will get up first to prepare breakfast, so it is best I sleep downstairs."

Verlie Eva Miller

Every night another guest or two arrived. Kind neighbors offered lodging, and eventually everyone was bedded down. It was just like old times. Ted and his bride-to-be didn't mind a bit; all the noise and activity seemed to make the days go by faster. Rehearsal was on Friday evening. It went so smoothly you would think they were professionals. Hanna Marie had practiced in her dreams over and over through the years.

The day dawned, and relatives insisted they were all going into town before the wedding to try out the new restaurant, leaving Hanna some privacy in which to prepare herself for her big day. Hanna Marie took her wedding clothes to the church basement early, making sure that Ted's first glimpse would be when she marched down the aisle. She would dress in her old classroom, the walls still adorned with the oil cloth she had attached twenty-some years before.

Her suitcase was packed well in advance for the short, but sweet, honeymoon. Saturday the sun came up as predicted, but Hanna Marie declared it was the most unusual sunrise she had ever witnessed. The wedding was set for 2:00 p.m. to accommodate all the dairy farmers with their strict milking schedules. It would also give the bride and groom an earlier start on their wedding trip.

"Hi! What is Ted doing today? He left before he barely swallowed his coffee." It was Anna on the phone.

Hanna Marie knew where Ted was. She passed it off by saying, "I know he had a busy morning planned." Keeping a secret from her long time bosom pal was not easy.

It was good that the guests went out for breakfast. Hanna Marie barely had time to feed Buffy and pour herself some cornflakes. She swallowed some left over coffee and watered the plants. Next stop was to get her hair done, a luxury she often denied herself. Walking out of the shop, feeling like the queen of Sebeka, Hanna Marie stepped back to see over her bifocals. She could hardly believe her eyes. "Edith! Edith! My dear old schoolmate." They stared at each other and offered an embrace.

"We've only changed outwardly," Edith assured her old friend. "There is just a little more to love."

"Do you have time to have a bite to eat with me?" Hanna Marie was starved and nearly shaking. Both lunch and renewed friendship tasted so good. They gave each other a bear hug. "See you at church." The bride caught herself speeding. She arrived home to check on Buffy and hoped to at least get a glimpse of Ted.

About twelve o'clock Ted emerged from the machine shed and threw out a bucket of dirty water. He only waved at Hanna, thinking he was too dirty to even get near her. Besides he must hurry back to Anna's to bathe, dress, and do one more errand.

The church was freshly painted, inside and out. Fresh flowers had been placed behind the church on Hanna Marie's loved ones' graves. As she walked into the church to make a last minute check, she stood in awe. Never before had there been so many flowers on every windowsill. It was a garden of fragrance and color hanging and adorning every nook and corner. She gasped at the beauty and drank in the fragrance. Could this be a touch of heaven? Gazing in silence and breathing deeply, she knew she was not dreaming, and must get into her gown.

Anna knocked on her dressing room door. "I made lunch for Ted and Jussel, so I am a wee bit late. I never saw Ted so dirty as he was when he came into the house. Oh! This is the most beautiful gown you have ever created," Anna said as she aided in getting it over Hanna's beautiful hairdo. Where did you find those shoes?" Anna had never seen them before but then recalled hearing about them. The hat had been carefully preserved as though Mamma knew it would be worn at her daughter's wedding. Time did not stand still. The buttons on both gown and shoes were finally in place. Anna smoothed a lock of hair, stood back, and marveled at the living beauty.

"Anna, I hear the organ playing."

Assisting the bride with her long dress, Anna followed up the stairs to a side room. The groomsmen were in the front pew. Jussel whispered to Ted's son, Scott, "Where is Ted? He is never late for anything."

Five minutes before the hour Ted appeared on the scene with a rather flushed face. Ted's brother had the honor of playing the wedding march. Hanna Marie was almost breathless as she waited to feel the touch of Ted's strong arm. They had written their own personal vows. The entire ceremony was as unique as the bride and groom. When the minister pronounced them man and wife, you could hear a pin drop as the kiss of their pledge was sealed.

Leaving Father and Mother was not a problem for either the bride or groom, but they still mourned the loss of their parents and were praying somehow that they could get a glimpse of their sacred day.

Standing with the bridal party for the next half hour was gratifying. The guests were drawn to the basement by the aroma of coffee, ribbon sandwiches, dainty cookies, and, of course, the wedding cake. The tables were covered in a rainbow of pastel colors. Centerpieces were antique teapots, many from Finland.

Two nephews that usually would be the first in the food line were up to mischief. Lifting a gunnysack filled with cans of brick cheese and old lipstick, they looked for Ted's car. "Which car shall we attack?" Perplexed, they decided to get in the reception line and listen for clues.

"Do you know where Ted's car is?" was the question that no one could answer.

Three hours had past and it was time for the farm families to leave for their barns when a stylish buggy drove into the

Behind the Mirror

churchyard. It was gaily decorated with ribbons and bows, with bells hanging from the sides. A man held the lines that guided the Belgian team. Their tails were tied in perfect knots; the harness was polished to a spit shine. The horse's manes were brushed and trimmed. With a swallow-tail suit and a black hat, the driver looked the part. He alighted and handed Papa's Stetson hat to Ted as he escorted the bride and groom to the rear seat of the carriage. The crowd gathered, cameras clicked; laughter, clapping, and whistling filled the air.

Hanna Marie in Mamma's shoes and hat made it all picture perfect. Ted and Hanna waved to the crowd. The obedient horses took off. The bride and groom had planned to go around one square mile. Every car quickly lined up, following the four-mile parade. The horns were blaring as they turned into the old farmstead.

The buggy was put in the shed, the horses unharnessed and watered, and the chauffeur drove a brand new Buick up to the front door. He alighted to open the rear door for Ted and Hanna Marie. Now in their going-away attire, the bride in a deep purple suit, and Ted dressed to the hilt in his wedding gray pinstripe suit, they were ready to conquer the world. The driver took them as far as his home in Sebeka, then Ted saddled into the driver's seat, whisking them off to the bridal suite. It had been reserved since the big furniture-shopping day.

CHAPTER 19

The Honeymoon

Anna and Jussel were trying to settle down after a very full week. Relatives were now journeying back to their homes.

"Well, Ted will no longer be our weekend guest," mourned Anna, who had grown to love her new brother-in-law.

"Oh, Anna, he is only going to be a stone's throw away."

"Now I know why Ted was so busy this morning and how he got so unearthly dirty."

"Yeah, cleaning up that old, retired buggy after all those years must have been a dirty job," agreed Jussel.

"Where do you figure he found that chauffeur?"

It was not only the topic in Anna's bedroom that night. It was the talk of the town for several weeks. Everyone in the neighborhood repainted a picture in various verbal colors of the unusual wedding departure.

The bride and the groom feared they would wake up and discover they were dreaming. Their youth and their spirits had been renewed as the eagle's. God had rewarded them for being faithful to the tasks he had laid out for them during the illnesses of their loved ones.

Beginning the day with a prayer of thanksgiving, they left to find a place to worship. Would anyone ever guess they were newlyweds in a strange church?

Verlie Eva Miller

"Good morning! You know, you two look like the happiest couple I have ever met," an elderly man delivered the complement along with a hearty handshake. "You must be new in our fair city."

"We are just visiting." Ted attempted casual speech as best he could as they were escorted to front of the church. It was a fine sermon, but these newlyweds had a difficult time concentrating, and the text slipped right past them.

Recalling the day they hunted for furniture, they were soon on their way to a place that served wonderful food. Visiting Paul Bunyan was next on their agenda. They registered as Mr. & Mrs. Ted Palarmore.

"Well, who should be strolling in our park today? None other than the bride and groom," said the man on the loudspeaker.

An amazed couple wondered *how in the world does Paul Bunyan know us?* They were unaware that a man from Sebeka was on duty that very weekend.

Exploring northern Minnesota entertained them for an entire week. Listening to the roar of Lake Superior on the mighty rocks along North Shore Drive, the two lovers continued sharing plans for their future. They were simply enjoying life perhaps as much as any couple could.

"All good things must come to an end, except honeymoons. We'll carry on when we head south for the winter and keep it going ever after." Ted was confident. They were packing slowly to the sound of the waves on the shore, not rushing the moments. Ted drew Hanna Marie close. "We will celebrate wherever we are. Getting a late start, we must enjoy every day God grants us."

Buffy had been boarding with Anna and Jussel. Could she ever forgive her mistress for deserting her? Her rations were untouched the first three endless days. Anna tried to reassure her that Hanna would return. The week did end, and Anna

Behind the Mirror

took Buffy home. Gathering the accumulated mail and Buffy's dish, she walked the half-mile. Buffy ran ahead as fast as her short little legs could carry her. Scratching on the door to the tune of a soft whine, the door opened and in shot Buffy. She skidded on the freshly polished floors, took a tumble or two as she exceeded the speed limit making the corners. Sniffing soon turned into an insistent bark at the stairway door. Hanna Marie had to be upstairs. Gaining access to the stairs, within minutes Buffy returned with one of her mistress' shoes.

As Anna watered the violets, she recalled that nieces had slept in the new bed. Luckily she found a set of queen size sheets among the gifts. A smirk crossed her face, recalling the short-sheeted bed she and Jussel tried to crawl into after their honeymoon. She could never remember having so much fun making a bed.

"I better hurry," she confided in Buffy. Buffy was still exploring every nook as she sensed something strange about to transpire. Anna rushed out so fast that she caught her skirt in the door and had to unlock it once more. "Come on, Buff!" There was no way that Buffy was going to leave that porch. She plunked herself down, facing the road from the top step. Her hour of vigilance proved to pay off. A strange car drove in.

"No one will cross this threshold as long as I am on guard duty," Buffy said to the intruders in no uncertain canine terms. Ted stepped out of the car and Buffy came scooting around the other side to greet Hanna Marie. Gently opening the door, Ted's princess slipped out. Trying to decide if she was mad or glad, Buffy burst into a run as they stood admiring the fall trees. She ran in circles around them before leaping in the air. After Hanna stroked and praised her, she settled down on the porch rug and pondered the length of Ted's stay. "When will I have Hanna Marie all to myself?" Buffy's face seemed to demand.

Verlie Eva Miller

Ted unloaded the suitcases before putting the Buick in the machine shed beside the buggy. Returning to help unpack the suitcases, he paused as though he were dreaming. Buffy was suspicious to discover Ted hanging his clothes in the master bedroom. She did not intend to share Hanna Marie with anyone on a full-time basis. Her mistress comforted her with a gentle stroke. "You will learn to love him, too, Buff."

The newlyweds were weary from travel. A cup of tea hit the spot while chatting over plans for the morrow and the tomorrows.

"We have to buy lumber for the picket fence."

"And groceries. Those nieces and nephews of mine nearly ate us out of house and home."

Carefully removing the spread, the twosome admired the new set. The quilt that Mamma had stitched for Hanna Marie had never been out of the closet until now. Hanna dreamed of the day she would use it.

Having never slept in Mamma's bedroom since she was a child, the scene surfaced of a little girl diving in between Mamma and Papa during a storm. She felt the warmth of Mamma's body and heard the comforting words of Papa. "God will take care of you, dear!"

Ted questioned the serious countenance on his bride's face.

"Oh, I was recalling the last time I slept in this room when I was a small child. Nothing can dampen my first night here with you, my love."

Preparation for bed and a short prayer before hopping in was interrupted with laughter as they tried to get their feet to the foot of the bed.

"Someone has been having fun," Hanna recalled doing the same thing to Anna and Jussel many years before.

Meanwhile, Buffy was trying to figure out why Hanna Marie could not find her way upstairs. She put up a fuss until

Behind the Mirror

Hanna reluctantly placed her basket by their bedroom door. During the night there were intervals of whispers that ruffled every nerve in Buff's furry body.

Dressed for the day, complete with shave and hair in place (though still wet), Ted grabbed his wife's apron. It was the most memorable picture that a woman in love ever snapped in her scanty nightgown. Little did she realize how many times she would gaze at this picture and relive precious memories.

Rushing back to dress, Hanna could hardly wait to join Ted for breakfast. She was amazed at the arrangements of fall flowers that complemented the setting, and all she could do was beam.

"There is no place like home," echoed in the walls. Ted could never have felt more at home than at this historical moment. Buffy was settled under the table and did a perfect job of vacuuming up every crumb from her new Master's table.

The newlyweds spent more time gathering materials for the fence project their first full day. Indian summer was very cooperative. The day was sunny and bright. Ted laid out the position of the fence. Stretching twine, he stood back and admired how straight that fence line would be.

"I hate to go in and make supper; I would much rather help dig fence post holes," Hanna lamented. She was reminded of how she tagged behind Papa when she was about seven years old as he dug in the turf. She recalled how fresh the earth felt on her bare feet.

Ted gave his bride a kiss on her forehead and thanked her for her helpful suggestions.

"Darling, I am so hungry, and I am terribly tired of peanut butter sandwiches." It was still fresh on Ted's mind how disappointing it was to go into an empty kitchen and scrounge around for something to eat. He had to admit he had been waited on hand and foot until about a year and half ago. Now he was eager to work up an appetite. Hanna was capable of preparing that tasty meal and cheerfully called him in for supper.

CHAPTER 20

Heidi and Karl

Karl's pleasant years with Heidi could fill an entire book. Four children were special gifts that invaded their home and conquered their hearts. Karl pursued his goal and became a commercial pilot, safely carrying trusting passengers to their destination year after year. His dream to own a plane of his own was fulfilled. Living far from his childhood home, it proved to be a blessing. Holidays found the family landing at the small airport in Wadena. As the children grew and established homes of their own, Heidi and Karl were often alone on trips.

One day Karl felt an urgent need to visit Bert, an old army buddy who lived in Pennsylvania. Bert's hopes for tomorrow were fading. He had to see him, just one more time.

Heidi decided to stay home on this trip, not wanting to miss welcoming a new grandchild whose due date was already past. Kissing Heidi good-bye was not getting any easier with age. The car was running, and he did not have any an item to retrieve, but still he wanted to give her one more squeeze and lingering kiss. She was usually right by his side for trips like this.

The weather report was perfect for flying that day. He recalled the storms he and his buddy Bert had encountered over enemy territory, but this trip east went off without

Verlie Eva Miller

problems. His visit with his friend was filled with mixed emotions. "I had to see you again, Bert. I had to be sure you will meet me in heaven."

"You need not worry about that, Karl. Observing your walk with Christ all those years has greatly influenced my life. I have my reservation made for eternity. I could not face these days without that hope and assurance."

They talked of how God had protected them the time two engines were damaged, forcing their last-second bailout. They caught up on the busy years they spent raising their families.

Karl knew Bert's voice was softening and his weary look prompted Karl to move on and give Bert time to spend with his wife and family. They were kind to give him this time alone with his dear friend. They embraced, shed a few tears on each other's shoulder, and Karl returned to the airport by cab. The weather report for the return trip warned of storms. Karl normally did not take chances, but this time he wavered.

"I must get back. I have to take off for Hawaii tomorrow; the airline is counting on me."

Karl never dreamed how soon he and Bert would have an eternity to visit and celebrate.

Heidi recovered from her flu bug and busied herself going through old photographs. She relived her entire life in the process and counted how blessed she was to have Karl by her side in so many pictures. Bedtimes were lonely without her lover to cheer her. It was two a.m. when she awoke from a nightmare. It was as if a dark cloud was soaring over her very bed. Claiming God's promises that He was in charge of their lives gave her peace that passed all understanding. She committed Karl to the Lord. As the cloud was lifted, Heidi was soon in a peaceful sleep until four a.m. when the call came from her daughter.

Behind the Mirror

"Mom, I am at the hospital, I hated to call you at this hour but you made me promise I would. I don't think it will be long before the baby comes. You decide if you want to make a trip at this early hour."

Of course Heidi was wide-awake and into her clothes in minutes. She combed through her now graying hair and thought, *I really look more like a Grandma every day!*

"Oh, how I wish Karl could be here."

A bouncing baby boy was exercising his lungs by the time Grandma arrived. He had blazing red hair and fair skin. A flash back of a baby picture that she had dusted over the years left an indelible mark.

"The very splitting image of Karl," were the first words Heidi uttered. Giving Brenda a big kiss, she asked, "Have you decided on a name?"

"Yes, his other Grandpa is Thomas. Meet Thomas Karl. Tommy it will be."

The new papa stood at the head of the bed wiping the mother's brow, grinning from ear to ear.

Heidi wanted to call the proud new grandpa. He should be home by now. Perhaps he's sleeping. She remembered he had to fly out tomorrow. She tried again and when she could not get him, she decided to return home. Kissing the new mommy, and longingly gazing at little Tommy in the nursery, she left, promising to come back. The phone was ringing on her arrival home with the fatal report of a plane crash. Karl was gone.

The family members met at the little, red Lutheran church for a private service at the church the family had attended since the day it was built. It had been a long week waiting to finalize the complicated arrangements. Heidi boarded a plane to make the painful trip back east. It did give Brenda a little time to recover from such an emotional week and pack to take her precious bundle for his first plane ride.

Verlie Eva Miller

Brenda wondered if he, like his Grandpa, would someday be a pilot. It was decided that the church could not take care of the large crowd. The service would be held in Wadena at the very place Karl's high school graduation exercise was held. How fitting, his schoolmates concluded.

Cars were parked around every block. Never in the history of Sebeka had so many former residents returned for such a homecoming. Schoolmates that had drifted to other states found time to pay their last respects to someone they loved and admired so highly.

One of Karl's former schoolmates was now the pastor of the little red church. He was now fifty and had conducted many funeral services but none so touching and difficult as the service that faced him now. One of Karl's cousins sang his favorite hymns in a golden voice, "I Will Meet You In The Morning" and "Sweet Hour Of Prayer." Family and friends paid tributes before the Pastor delivered a message that cut to the very heart of each one.

The first row was filled with Heidi, her children, their mates, and her grandchildren. Behind them, cousins with families and the now aging Jussel and Anna sat as though in a bad dream. Ted and Hanna Marie sat in the third row with her siblings, thinking of Karl now perhaps embracing his Grandpa and Grandma. She whispered to Ted, "I never thought I would outlive my dear Karl." She had handed the Pastor an envelope the night before, and was waiting to see what he decided to do with it.

"In conclusion I would like to read a speech that Karl delivered on this very spot." It was the speech that Grandma had tucked away with her dearest treasures.

As the sun was setting, family members met at the old homestead. Hanna Marie sat in Papa's old rocker and held little Tommy close to her heart, thinking to herself, *"The Lord giveth and taketh away."* Her heart was bleeding and yet she rejoiced over the replica that God had sent the very night of the plane crash.

The memories of that scene were too painful to write in her journal. As time eventually subdues the sting, she determined the day would come when she could pen her thoughts without flooding the parchment.

CHAPTER 21

Another Painful Good-bye

Five years disappeared as a blade of grass. Ted and Hanna Marie counted each day as a special gift. Only once did Ted leave the house without a peck on the cheek; he traipsed halfway to the mailbox and stopped dead still. "I forgot to tell my dear Hanna goodbye." He retraced his tracks. Hanna was pulling weeds in the garden.

"Boy did you make fast work of that trip. Where is the mail? I didn't know it was a holiday." She finally took a deep breath and gave Ted time to explain, kiss her goodbye and head off for the mail again. Hanna Marie wiped her forehead; told Buffy to get out of the garden; and tried to figure out men, thinking he could have just apologized when he returned.

When Ted returned his face seemed flushed, and he was a little out of breath. He handed Hanna her personal letter and headed for the swing to catch up on world affairs. The *Fergus Falls Journal* reported not only news but smelled of home gossip, too.

Ted was spending more time on the porch swing than usual. Hanna would say to herself, "It is just not like him to not help me in the garden more. He never complains of pain. His old hearty appetite is not the same; I try to cook his favorite foods." That night Hanna Marie confronted him about his health. "Are you feeling all right, dear?"

"Well, I suppose I am just showing signs of old age, but I hate to admit it."

"I think you should have a check up, just to be safe."

Ted, like all proud men, did not think that necessary. Hanna Marie did not belabor the subject. She expressed her love and concern. They kissed goodnight and rolled over on their respective sides of the bed.

The next day Ted determined to display a little more vitality in his steps. It was a typical hot Minnesota day in late summer. In the afternoon, Ted insisted on completing the hoeing of the potatoes.

"Darling, let's wait until morning. It should be a little cooler," insisted Hanna.

Ted was not in the habit of leaving jobs half done. Besides, he wanted to prove to his wife that he was okay. He took a big drink of water and gave Hanna the tightest hug and lingering kiss she had remembered since the honeymoon. "I love you so much." For good measure he gave a final peck on her forehead.

Hanna Marie hurried with the lunch dishes. She had finally adopted Ted's terminology for the noon meal; "dinner" it had always been before Ted came around, but now it was officially termed "lunch."

She sat in Papa's chair, slipped off her shoes, and sneaked a peek at the funnies in the *Fergus Falls Journal*.

"Oh, my goodness sakes alive! I must have fallen asleep."

She hurriedly put on her shoes, grabbed her straw hat and garden gloves and headed for the garden. She could not see Ted. Only a scarecrow stood above the sweet corn. She rushed to the potato patch on the other side of the corn.

Behind the Mirror

Buffy sensed the tenseness in her mistress' voice and ran through the garden gate ahead of her. Ted was flat between the rows.

"Ted! Ted, my Darling! Ted, please answers me. I love you so much. Please don't leave me now." Hanna Marie was down on her knees. Ted moaned and tried to raise himself. She labored to turn his body. Buffy could only offer a sympathetic whine while licking Ted's hand. Feeling a faint pulse and knowing she could not lift Ted, Hanna Marie rushed to the phone and called the doctor before calling Anna.

"Anna! I can't believe this, but I am afraid Ted has suffered a heart attack. I will go back to the garden until help arrives." By the time Hanna returned to the garden with a glass of water and a cold cloth for Ted's brow, he revived and asked, "What happened? What happened?"

"You must have had a heat stroke. Ted, I am so happy to hear your voice." Hanna continued to cool him and offer him sips of water.

The doctor left his patient in his office and was by Ted's side in minutes. Ted's pulse was fast but regular. "I think it is from the extreme heat." Jussel arrived just in time to help the strong doctor carry him to his bed. Buffy followed under their feet, with Anna and Hanna right behind. "Do keep Ted in bed until tomorrow, and give him a very light supper."

The doctor remained for a couple of hours to be sure Ted was out of danger, making sure his blood pressure and pulse were normal. Anna stayed for soup and rye bread. They put up the folding table at the bedside and supped with Ted. Ted joined in the dialogue and of course the content was the hot weather and the precautions older folk must take. Ted admitted he should have listened to Hanna. Anna left with a much lighter heart than she had after the urgent phone call.

"Call me anytime of the day or night," and with that she was closing the screen door.

Hanna and Ted had serious thoughts about separation and the need to discuss such sobering subjects. They spent an hour or so doing just that. Then assuring each other how deep their affections were, they embraced once more. Sleep overtook them as they both muttered, "Good-ni...."

It was nearly three in the morning when Hanna awoke and rehearsed the garden scene in her mind. She gently rolled over to place her arm around Ted. His body was cold. Hanna jumped from her bed and ran for the phone.

The doctor confirmed her fears and Hanna walked as in a daze. When she could collect the reality of it all, she recalled Ted telling her just hours before, "At the end of my journey here, I don't think it matters where I rest. I will be resting in the arms of Jesus. If I should die before you, consult my children. I do have space beside Lill."

The family rushed to Hanna Marie's side. Ruth and Scott talked for hours into the night. "Mother is not in that grave. She is with our little brother and now Dad," Scott reasoned.

"Daddy loved the country. It will be much easier for us to visit here than for Hanna Marie to come to the city," Ruth added.

The next morning they found Hanna Marie out picking a bouquet from Ted's beautiful garden. She came to the gate and stared at the white picket fence. Her memories of the first day together on the farm flashed before her as yesterday. She held her bouquet as though it was part of the flesh and blood of the gardener. "How could I have any more tears?" She admitted how long the night had been. Scott held her tenderly.

Ted's body was placed not far from Ade and Greta. Hanna Marie walked away with many emotions. God was so good to give her the most beautiful five years that any bride could dream of. Humanly speaking she longed for it to

Behind the Mirror

endure forever. Still in a state of shock and having tasted this bitter pill before, she knew that God would see her through the days ahead. As she dropped a flower on his open grave she softly cried, "Someday I will be with you forever, Ted."

The four grandchildren lingered in the background. They had learned to love their new grandmother and had spent a week or two each summer on the farm. They rode the horses, played in the haymow, and even took the buggy out for a spin once in a while. Picking wild berries with Grandpa, storing hazelnuts on top of the chicken coop to dry, and picnics at the source of the Mississippi were memories that would remain forever. Death touched them deeply, and they missed Grandma Lill keenly at a time like this.

Ruth and Scott remained the entire week. Hanna Marie requested that they take any clothing or personal belongings that they would like. Scott took a couple of Ted's suits, making sure to leave his wedding suit.

"Don't forget to check through his tools in the shed, and I think you two should decide about the car."

"We would never think of taking that car," Scott and Ruth responded simultaneously. "You will need a car."

Hanna Marie did not plan on doing much traveling, besides she still had the old family thirty-six Chevrolet.

The day for departure came. The family met in the parlor. Hanna Marie sat in Papa's chair. Scott and Ruth's families gathered around. Scott broke the silence with a sincere prayer for comfort and protection for Grandma Hanna. How much his voice sounded like Ted's, and his faith was just as strong. Scott had said good-bye, and she remained standing as long as she could see the car.

Buffy cuddled closely to Hanna's slacks, as if making the profound statement, "Hanna you still have me."

Blotting her tears, Hanna slowly trudged to the porch. She sat on the swing that Ted had painted to match the fence and was lost in a sea of memories. One hour passed and darkness penetrated her world. "Oh, Teddy, I miss you! I miss you!" she cried out loud. Buffy hopped on the swing beside her.

Coming back to the real world, Hanna patted Buffy and decided it was time to go to bed. The house was dark. Hanna was so thankful that she did not have to hunt for a match and a lamp. A flip of the switch and a positive thought flooded her mind for just a moment.

"Another adjustment," Hanna whispered under her breath. Secretly wishing she had a bad dream. Ted's departure was without warning. Mamma and Daddy had displayed and talked of failing health. Hanna had endeavored to prepare for their death.

She plopped herself on the edge of the bed and a chill passed over her like a streak of lightning. Ted was her warming oven; where would she put her cold feet tonight? Scott and his wife had slept in the bed since Ted's departure and Hanna Marie had gone back up to her old room. They remarked that there was a warm spot on Dad's side of the bed. Hanna was too numb to think they were serious. She knew it would be best to sleep downstairs in the lonely old house. Moving Buffy's basket into her bedroom added a bit of life and comfort. Hanna joined her lone companion when the kitchen was in order.

Hanna tossed and turned, then reaching the other side of the bed she felt the warm spot, thinking that was just the spot where Ted's heart would have been positioned. She thought she must be dreaming. Awake until morning, she reached over. *I cannot tell a soul about this, Lord, but I believe it is a promise that Ted will always be with me in spirit. I may as well stay downstairs tonight. It won't be any easier tomorrow night*, she reasoned.

CHAPTER 22

More Adjustments

Enjoying married life to its fullest, Hanna Marie did not in her wildest dreams anticipate being alone in five and one half short years. Hanna spoke aloud, "It is morning, and I am a widow. Please God, help me to take one day at a time and lean on you."

It wasn't fun to make pancakes for one person. The excitement of a new day had evaporated. She went through the mechanics of keeping soul and body together. The days were long; at low moments the lonely bride wondered if she could go on. She found comfort in feeding her inner life on the Bread of Life, her favorite book. Her appetite was sadly lacking, though the clock on the wall reminded her it was lunch time or should she call it dinner again? *No, in memory of you, Ted, it will be lunch.* In one month the scale was short ten pounds. *I don't mind losing weight, but not this way. I do wish Ted could see me now.*

After new sod was rolled on Ted's grave, Hanna Marie took the last of the fall roses to deposit as a token of her love. Today she felt like the last rose of summer herself. The tombstone had just been carefully put in place. The roses, in contrast with the deep green sod, gave new life to the landscape. The maple trees surrounding the church property, sprinkled among the stalwart pine, added a finishing touch of fall with their colorful leaves. Hanna stood in silence, head and heart bowed before her Wonderful Maker.

Dear Jesus,

A long period of silence prevailed before she could continue.

> *Somehow I can see Ted in a garden of beauty, worshipping you. I cannot go to him; I thank you that I have an audience with you. Please allow Ted to know that I miss him. I have not lost faith. Thank you for the five memorable years we enjoyed together. Help me to find my way. Help me to fulfill every purpose in life that you have assigned to me until the dead in Christ shall rise and we who are alive will meet together.*

She lingered long on her knees, pausing often to drink in the beauty of her surroundings as memories surfaced. Recalling the first day Ted worshipped with her in the church, the wedding, and the triumphant departure in the polished buggy. She could just hear the laughter from wedding guests. Thoughts of Ted's strong arm around her brought comfort even now.

She put mixed bouquets on all her loved ones' graves, pausing in silent reflection. Hanna Marie left with a lighter heart, more determined than ever to keep pressing on. She stopped by Anna and Jussel's, unaware that it was time for lunch.

"You must have a bite to eat with us," Anna insisted.

"I did not realize that I have spent two hours at the cemetery."

Behind the Mirror

The kitchen aroma made it impossible to refuse that invitation. Just to have someone to converse with was food for her soul. They talked of times together, of the day Ted cleaned up the old buggy and of the short sheets on their first night in the farmhouse as the dishes were being done.

Hanna Marie headed on home stopping to check the hazelnuts and watch a squirrel who was making sure she had her share of the nuts stashed away. He peeked back with his cheeks so stuffed that he could not let out a squeak.

Buffy met her mistress at the door in a rush to get out and water just about anything. She earned an apology, "I didn't plan to leave you so long."

Perhaps Buffy was worried that Hanna Marie had been out looking for a new partner. She would have been comforted if only Hanna could assure her that thought would never enter her mind. Living with Ted had fulfilled all those longings. He had even provided her with children and grandchildren that loved her as their own. The feeling was mutual. Every day a little more normalcy worked its way into her lonely life. There were times when Hanna Marie would catch herself thinking *I must tell Ted what I found or did*, only to sink back with the realization that he was out of reach. At times, she almost set the table for two and called him in to eat lunch.

Trying to sleep in the big bed alone, Hanna Marie rolled on one side, then another, then flat on her back but to no avail. She could not get to sleep. Hanna lie awake all night again, missing Ted so desperately. With no sheep to count, her mind drifted off to a scene that had touched her past. She had taken Ted through the entire episode one night when they could not get to sleep. It was not long after the marriage began.

She was never able to go into detail before as her voice always choked up. "If we are just going to lie here and toss,

Verlie Eva Miller

I think it is as good a time as I will ever find to tell you more than I told you in my letter." After Ted had burned it, he never pressed Hanna for a detailed account. Hanna had finally decided Ted deserved more. Ted was wide awake as she proceeded to tell him the entire story, the defining moment in her early adult years that changed the course of history. She talked softly as though some listening ear was just outside the bedroom door.

CHAPTER 23

The Great Unveiling

Reliving the night she revealed to Ted the secrets of her past, she was lost in a world that seemed far remote from the years that followed. It was all so vivid now. She had buried her past in the recesses of her heart to protect her loved ones.

Hanna relived her story as she told it to Ted.

"No young man had ever paid much notice to me during my school years. Graduating from high school without having done much dating, I never really thought about marriage. A career was on my mind, and I went to the big city to seek my fortune, or at least my bread and butter.

"I had just returned home for a week's vacation, and it was fun to get home again. How I had missed the sauna that Papa built. Water from a spring was piped down to the building into a large barrel that was heated with a wood fire along with the rocks. No one else in the neighborhood

Verlie Eva Miller

had such a luxury. On Saturday nights we attracted many neighbors and often had potluck suppers.

"First the children all bathed. The fire was stoked to provide heat to burn the toxins out of the whole neighborhood. Water was splashed over the hot rocks. After chores, the men gathered their towels and swimming gear. Later that evening, I, now at the age of twenty-two, joined some of the women. They added clean water, waited for it to heat and chatted on and on, while splashing water on the hot rocks. One by one, they all said good night and left. I enjoyed it so much that I lingered by myself. I splashed and bathed in luxury. When I opened my eyes there stood a young man from Michigan that had been visiting his Auntie Anna, my sister-in-law. He was too bashful to bathe with other men or boys and planned to sneak over after everyone else had finished. He stood in his swimming suit, towel and soap in hand. He was as surprised as I was.

"I grabbed my towel and he rushed out, embarrassed also. I put on my robe and moccasins and peeked out the door.

"'I am sorry to barge in,' he confessed when I went out the door. 'I just expected the place to be vacant by now.' I had seen Tom when he visited his Aunt and Uncle each summer. We only met at church or at picnics. I was as bashful as he was.

"As we visited in the cool evening air, my wet hair prompted me to go back into the sauna building. Tom followed me. He was lonesome and had not met anyone his own age all week. We talked on and on before saying good night. The following Saturday night I waited until I thought all bathers had left. I wanted one last sauna before leaving for the big city on Sunday. To my surprise, there was Tom, completely dressed. His red hair was wet, slicked down, some masculine scent floating through the air, and bashful Tom all smiles. He was waiting for his hair to dry before going out in the cool evening breeze.

"I greeted him in friendly manner, and asked if he would mind leaving. "I would visit with you, but I am anxiously awaiting my sauna before the stones and fire cool down."

"'Would you mind if I go for a walk and return later? I will be down by the lake. Just whistle if you care to go for a walk.'

"I did not take the leisurely steam bath I had planned. When did I ever have a chance to visit or go for a walk with such a handsome young man? The cold rinse woke me up to the reality that I would have to walk in my long robe. Deciding not to let that dampen my spirits, I gave out a shrill whistle. Tom was only a stone's throw away and was soon by my side.

"'Shall we walk on the road or would you prefer the path to the lake?'

"I was thrilled beyond words. A moment of silence passed before I could utter, 'Let's go down by the lake.'

"An owl in the distance was calling his mate. Squirrels were scampering behind the trees. They expected to have the trail to themselves by dusk. Tom talked of his home life and family as if earning the right to tell me more intimate things.

"'I have been thinking and dreaming of you all week, Hanna Marie. I could not think of any other way to see you again. Please forgive me for being so bold as to blurt all this out so soon. Auntie told me you will be leaving tomorrow, and I wonder if you would be so kind as to give me your address.'

"I reached for his extended hand and we strolled back. We talked until I felt a chill come over me; my thick hair was still damp.

"'I think I will have to go back and stand by the hot rocks to dry my hair.'

"'Do you mind if I keep you company?'

"'Not at all.'

"I had never had such wonderful companion in my twenty-two years.

"I felt as though I had known Tom all my life. I reached in my basket for my hairbrush. Leaning over the heated rocks, I brushed my long hair.

"'I should have done this before the walk, but I thought it would get dark too soon,' I admitted to Tom.

"Tom admired my hair as he ventured closer and ran his fingers through it. 'Your brown curls are the most beautiful locks I have ever touched. Forgive me for being so bold, I have been dreaming about you day and night since last Saturday. How can I tell you my deepest thoughts when I have known you for such a short while? I would wait, but I do not know when our paths will cross again.'

"He lifted my hair away from my face and asked me for a kiss. I thought I was dreaming. When had anyone wanted a kiss from me? I responded by silently looking up into his eyes. My heart melted. We talked as darkness closed in upon us. No one had ever touched me with such tenderness. It was time to say goodnight, and I suggested it halfheartedly.

"Then it happened. A lingering kiss brought temptations that neither had ever been warned to guard against. Parents never covered that forbidden subject. Tom cried and asked my forgiveness. I acknowledged that I was unprepared for a night filled with such staggering and scandalous surprises, the solitude, the twilight, then darkness, and moments that neither had ever experienced. These were no excuses for two grown people to yield to temptation. Yet that one moment, just a fleeting, blissfully blind-sighted moment, changed the course of my life forever.

Behind the Mirror

"'I can't blame you alone, Tom.' I knew that I should have been more prepared for temptation. With that I broke into convulsive crying. We pledged secrecy and prayed together for God's forgiveness. It was pitch dark when we returned to the farmhouse doorsteps. We sat on the swing in silence. Tom reached for my hand and kissed it gently.

"Sunday morning, two demur and abashed young people were seated across the aisle from each other in church, each silently praying for reassurance that God had forgiven them. Tom hurried to catch up with me after a sermon on the disobedient servant. Tom handed me a slip of paper with his home address in Michigan.

"'I am on my way back to Minneapolis. I will never forget you and will write soon.' It finally dawned on us that we would be leaving on the same bus. Tom's Auntie offered to take me to Wadena, unaware of the extent of our friendship, its passion and its sorrow.

"I was very quiet over the noon meal. Mamma and Daddy concluded it was a touch of homesickness. Oblivious to all that had transpired in the past few hours, they had been sleeping soundly when I crept into my bed the night before. Now as I left my home, I knew I was leaving behind much more. I gave Mamma a kiss and shook Daddy's hand, avoiding their eyes, trying not to reveal the confusion in my soul or the pain in my countenance.

"The long bus ride together was a bonus that we never expected. It gave us time to get to know each other, a bit about our life history, and to share a few words of affection, in spite of our shame. The four and one half hour ride was history before we could blink our eyes. Tom told me of his dream to become a doctor and then return to his small town in Michigan. He was saving every penny to complete college.

"'When I have a degree in my hand, I will return and propose to you. I hope to see you many times before then. I will always wait for you. Don't forget me. Be sure to write,' Tom pleaded as he returned to the departing bus. He waited until the last minute to board it. The bus roared away, leaving me more alone than I had ever felt. I never saw him again."

Hanna Marie took a big sigh and was so relieved that she finally made it through the entire episode without weeping. Ted had only known what the note contained. He never questioned further. He was sure Hanna Marie would enlarge on the story someday. The note read:

> *My Darling Ted,*
>
> *I am sorry I could not tell you this without breaking down. I was actually glad that we had to rush off to catch the bus that day. Before I say,"I do" to you my love, I need to confess that though never married, I gave birth to a child. I was twenty-three at the time.*
>
> *I have found fulfillment in caring for my parents until I met you. I did not dream that I would ever meet someone that would want to marry me. I cannot tell you more now. If this should change how you feel about me I will understand and try to go on without you. I have sworn to secrecy about this child. Wonderful parents have adopted him.*
>
> *Please forgive me for not disclosing this chapter of my life earlier. Perhaps if your proposal is without regret, I will disclose the details of the darkest hour of my life at some later date.*
>
> *Loving You Always,*
Hanna Marie

After bidding Tom goodbye at the bus station in

Behind the Mirror

Minneapolis, Hanna returned to her job a changed young woman. She was no longer looking forward to seeing the attractive co-worker, Ted. While she still secretly admired him, it was not the same after her incident with Tom.

Five weeks slipped by and then six. One morning she awoke with a nauseated feeling. She managed to make it through the next few weeks but did not improve. One long night, back in her apartment on the third floor, she could not live in denial another moment. She knew the price she paid for one weak moment. She could not bear to write to Tom. She did not care to interrupt his dream of becoming a doctor. She blamed herself.

First she wrote and confessed to her dear sisters. It was difficult to admit to her grave sin and deep regret. Two sisters came to her rescue but not before consulting their mother. They found a home for girls who were pregnant out of wedlock. They helped Hanna Marie pack her few belongings and shipped them back home. Hanna kept only what clothes fit her and moved into the large home in Minneapolis.

The dark cloud followed her to a very tiny, dreary room in a large old mansion. It was purchased for this specific need, and every room was in use. Unwed pregnancy was not as prevalent in those years as in subsequent generations, or perhaps it was better concealed, but the stigma it left was never lived down by the vulnerable young women on whom motherhood was thrust, nor on their parents and families. Mamma, Daddy and her sisters vowed never to reveal her secret shame to anyone. No one at home suspected anything; they were accustomed to seeing Hanna only about once a year, and no one in the big city took particular notice.

Hanna had much in common with her roommates down the halls. The matron assigned each one daily household duties, and they were each in charge of their laundry. Everyone had their turn with the paring knife and other tedious kitchen tasks. Hanna kept her good spirits and, looking on the bright side, was thankful for the extra training she received in housework and baking. She was soon appointed chief bread baker and room inspector.

She witnessed the delivery of several babies and began to dread her "fatal" day. The expectant mothers were urged to sign a statement, giving their newborns up for adoption immediately at birth. Hanna noticed that the mothers that held their babies were the ones that had the most difficult time letting go. With this observation in mind, she made a firm decision. *I will not sign that paper. I will only allow my baby to be placed in a foster home until I have time to think more clearly. I will never hold my baby or even glance at it. It* — she then began to wonder would it be a girl or a boy.

Sleeping on her hard bed at night gave her ample time to wonder. She prayed often for wisdom. When movement of real life stirred her very being, her heart ached for a husband and a home. She could not break down and write to Tom. He had written letters to her apartment only to find them in his own box the following week. She still could not bear to write to Tom. *If I would have exercised a bit of resistance I feel Tom would have done likewise. He would have had that much respect for me.* So on and on over the long weary months Hanna shouldered the blame, while her load became more cumbersome as each day dawned.

Mail time was either the highlight of the day or the lowest part of each day, depending on whether your name was called when mail was distributed. This day Hanna Marie's name was loud and clear. She ran to her room and tore a letter open with trembling hands.

> *My dear Sister,*
> *I am sorry we did not write last week. We were all so busy trying to help Daddy and be*

with Mamma in the hospital. We hesitated writing this news to you, when you are so crushed with your own problems. Mamma suffered a heart attack last week. She was in the Wadena Hospital for the entire week. The doctor suggests that she have complete rest for a long while. It did not do much damage to her heart. He strongly insisted on rest so it would not reoccur.

Mamma has been sewing for your little one. The flannel gown is so sweet. She also hemmed a few diapers by hand. I will mail them soon. Jussel and I envy you in a way. We have hoped for a little one for six years. So far it has been hopeless. When someone asks about you at church we simply tell him or her you are still in the big city.

We promise, dear Hanna, that we will never discuss your plight with anyone. It will always be our secret. We think of you daily and pray for you.
Love,
Anna and Jussel

Faint sobs drifted from that room as Hanna Marie felt a flood of guilt sweep over her. She knew the burden Mamma carried and the sorrow they all shared because of her missteps.

Soon it was Hanna Marie's turn to proceed to the delivery room. A kind old doctor came and assured her everything would be just fine. It will be hours before you need me. A few other waiting mothers gathered close by and whispered, "I'm so scared. I don't want to go through this," tears began to well up in her eyes.

"Well, there's not much we can do about that now, is there?" said her roommate, angry at the whole world. She had been taken advantage of, raped and then scorned by a distant relative.

The dark hours passed. The pain was almost unbearable but not as piercing as the emotional pain the new mother was enduring. If only she could have felt the support of an anxiously awaiting father. Hanna Marie finally heard the cry of her baby. His umbilical cord was tied and severed from his mother, perhaps never to connect with her again. The doctor examined the baby closely and returned to the mother to do repair work. The nurse then whisked the wee one away to put drops in his eyes, a tight band on his tummy, and dress the sweet little redhead in a flannel gown that Mamma had made.

Hanna Marie's wishes were carried out. The baby was rushed downstairs to the spacious foyer, where a basket, blanket and foster parents were waiting with a warm water bottle to prepare him for the cold reception and separation from the one that carried him next to her heart for nine long months.

"Do you care to know if the baby was a boy or girl?" the doctor asked cautiously. Hanna looked up with her red swollen eyes and nodded.

"It was a redheaded healthy little boy. He weighed seven pounds and two ounces." Hanna Marie gasped and began to weep. She wanted to scream "I want my little Tommy." Restraining herself caused her body to tremble, shaking the delivery table.

Hanna was as in agony for days. Her breasts were weeping for the one for whom they were supposed to provide sustenance. Food was brought to her room for two weeks. She could eat very little; her heart was breaking.

Other expectant mothers came to grill her with questions,

Behind the Mirror

seeking assurance and finding little. Some gave words of comfort; others came to say good-bye or to tell her how they would miss her wholewheat and rye bread. Some asked for her Finnish Pancake recipe, while others had the courage to ask the painful question, "Do you miss your baby?" Hanna could not answer; her countenance could not hide her pain.

Soon the matron informed her it was time to search for a job and an apartment of her own. She would not return to her old job.

Hanna Marie prayed for hours those long nights in the old mansion. Asking for guidance for her next move, divine inspiration came. Hanna Marie thought of Anna and Jussel and their longing for a child. She made a decision: *I want to go see Mamma before going back to work, and I must talk face to face with my brother.*

She headed home. Her head was spinning faster than the wheels on the Greyhound bus with an idea she felt was directly from the Lord. God could turn bad situations into blessings, and this was a golden opportunity to prove it. Her arms and heart still ached for her child. She hugged a pillow so tightly she thought the feathers might explode from the case. The pillow was soon dampened with tears.

Jussel met her at the depot. She wept at the very sight of a loved one. Jussel concealed his breaking heart to the best of his ability. He did grab Hanna's hand and held it briefly before placing it on the steering wheel. Then reaching for his red handkerchief, he blew his nose and said, "I think I am catching a cold."

Anna was out to greet her as they drove up. "Oh, we are so happy to see you!" A long embrace followed, and no one could talk.

"Anna and Jussel, I want you to know how much respect and love I have for you. I have a very special request to make. My child is a baby boy. I could not bear to look at him and

Verlie Eva Miller

then let him go, but the doctor told me was a red headed boy. So now you might as well know that your nephew Tommy is the father of my baby. I must get right to the point before I tell you more. Would you please adopt my baby?" She spoke with boldness, but voice breaking. "I promise I would never tell him or anyone that I am his mother; all I would ask is that I, as an auntie, would be permitted to see him often. Because of Mamma's illness I hope to remain at home and care for her. I cannot support the child and move home. I cannot take care of him and make my own way. This is the only course of action that will enable me to watch my son grow up. There is no one that will be better parents than you two." With those words she broke into sobs.

Jussel and Anna fell into each other's arms weeping. Hanna soon joined them. The threesome held each other for a time as though they were sealing the pact without verbal expression. They talked for a time until Hanna Marie remembered that Daddy and Mamma would be waiting for her.

Jussel took her home. He placed her suitcase on the back porch and quickly returned to his wife. He and Anna had much to talk over and celebrate. Hanna Marie needed to be alone with her parents. She rushed into the waiting arms of Mamma. After separations and heartaches, Mamma learned the comfort that a simple embrace affords. Daddy tipped his glasses back while wiping his eyes.

"Oh, my dear Hanna Marie, how my heart has ached for you," said Mamma.

When she regained her composure, a flood of questions poured from her lips. Hanna bravely answered them.

"Mamma, I could not look at my baby and then allow him to vanish from my arms. It was a seven-pound boy with red hair."

Mamma's faced turned white as she recalled the last time

Behind the Mirror

Hanna Marie was home, and vaguely recalled seeing her walking with the redheaded young man.

They talked of the long winter and of the heart attack. It took time for Mamma to get brave enough to ask where the baby was placed.

"He is at a foster home awaiting my decision. I have made the painful decision. Anna and Jussel are adopting my baby. I have made a solemn promise that I will never disclose to him or anyone that I am his mother. I will always be Auntie Hanna Marie, and will simply enjoy the privilege of seeing him often. May I move back home and care for you and Daddy in the coming years? I want to watch my baby, Anna and Jussel's son, grow up."

A big smile crossed Eli's face. Needing Hanna Marie now more than ever, Greta rocked in her chair in silence as she tried to take in this astonishing news. Jussel and Anna would be the parents, and, after going through the very shadows of despair, Hanna would hide in the background as an auntie. Eli sat in Papa's old, faded chair quietly amazed.

Greta apologized for the dust on the dining room table. "I have been so tired since my heart attack." Hanna Marie could see that Mamma was forced to neglect her housework and assured her she would not be returning to her job in Minneapolis. She hung her coat on the hook near the front door and ran for the dust rag. "There. That will make you feel better, Mamma."

It was time to get supper and the new maid grabbed her Mother's apron and took over as though she had always been on duty. Quietness hovered over the supper table.

When Jussel returned from taking Hanna home, he ran from the car leaving the door wide open. Anna was looking at the baby furniture in the Sears catalogue. He picked her up in his arms and twirled her until they were both dizzy.

Verlie Eva Miller

"How can we be so happy about this when my sister is so sad?"

"Jussel, dear, this is the only way we can help her under these tragic circumstances."

Wrestling over the situation after Jussel returned from milking, they again decided it was the only solution to their problems. Anna continued to make an order to Sears. Yards of flannel were on the list, baby bottles, and a bassinet.

They then called it a day. A banner day it was, though a sleepless night. *What shall we name our baby? When can we see him? Will we know how to properly feed and care for him?*

With hearts full of praise, they knelt together and thanked God for the awesome privilege of raising Hanna's little one. Two proud parents journeyed to the cities to sign adoption papers and claim their new son. Anna's heart pounded as she first touched the wee one. Wrapping him in the blanket that Mamma had crocheted for him, she gently picked him up and held his soft cheeks to her face. Jussel held him as though he may be a dream that would drift away any moment.

Hanna relived her entire life that night, often reaching to the other side of the bed, sleepily hoping she was dreaming. The bed was cold and lifeless except for one warm spot. It was the spot that Ted's heart had covered for five precious years. Hanna Marie was sure it could not be real. She now had one more secret she would be afraid to share. She felt for the place again and again. The message was loud and clear. Her Ted was reassuring her that everything was in the sea of God's forgiveness, his love was unchanging, and she fell asleep with new assurance that God would indeed provide beauty for ashes once more.

She determined that she could bury her sorrow by helping others. Church and community needs were abundant. Hanna

Behind the Mirror

Marie did not need to search to find them. Somehow they found her.

She lived for many years in the home that she loved so dearly. She marveled at the conveniences that Ted had added to the old farm home. The electric stove, the bathroom fixtures, the refinished floors, and the treasured picket fence, to name a few.

Months passed into years which finally took their toll on her health. Nieces and nephews came to her aid when she decided to move to a nursing home. Even while confined to living with others, she found words of comfort and a cup of cold water for those less fortunate.

That final call came just as she had prayed for. *Please God, just gently wake me from my sleep in your precious arms.* God granted that request. We are sure Jesus welcomed her and Ted was next in line.

Because she did not claim any offspring and her siblings had gone on before, nieces and nephews prepared the old farmstead for sale. Family members shared the furnishings that had been in the family since moving from Finland.

Everything was cleared out except for the attic. This sad job was left for the last. Grandmother's dress, Hanna Marie's wedding gown, Greta's button shoes, and her hat that Hanna Marie wore at her wedding were hanging in one corner. Under the octagon window was the old trunk. It was locked since the day Hanna sent it back home from the city by truck. She could never bear to turn the key. It was Pandora's box, and she had bolted those memories and hid the key.

"It won't budge. I had tried to open it so many times when I was a boy. It is jammed," said Hanna's nephew.

The search was on. They ran an extension cord down to Hanna Marie's room and connected an old lamp in the attic. Every rafter was gone over with a fine tooth comb, still no key. Finally one of the nephews screamed.

"I found it, I found it!"

He was down on his knees running his hand under the two by four that supported the window. The key had rusted from the dampness caused by the frost dripping from the window. Applying some oil, the key slipped into the hole and the great unveiling began.

There were letters from Tom, wrapped with a pretty red ribbon, and letters from Mamma and sisters. A 1923 calendar with dates marked: "Back at my apartment," "Letter from Tom today," "Quit my job today," "Moved to north Minneapolis," "Due date." These were some of many footnotes that revealed the secrets of Hanna Marie's heart.

There were a few dresses, dried flowers, and a little teacup that Papa had given her on her eighth birthday, wrapped in the hankie that Mamma had sent her for Christmas, 1923.

Jason held a silver compact high and said, "I wonder if this is of any value? I bet it is." He opened it and out fell a mirror, revealing a picture of Hanna Marie in the back of the lid.

"That hardly looks like her."

Jason's mother reached for the picture, then stared in silence. She had thought it unnecessary to tell Jason and his sisters this chapter of Hanna Marie's life.

"She was about to become a mother when this picture was taken."

Instead of getting to the bottom of the trunk that day Jason's mother had a long story to tell before satisfying his questions. She told how Anna and Jussel became the proud parents, how Aunt Anna was comforted to think there was some blood connection, and how cousin Karl fit perfectly into their family.

"The baby she gave birth to was your second cousin Karl. Aunt Hanna held her secret *behind the mirror*."